Dare to collect them all!

More books from The Midnight Library:
Nick Shadow's terrifying collection continues . . .

THE
MIDNIGHT
LIBRARY

—

The Whisperer

Nick Shadow

Hodder
Children's
Books

A division of Hachette Children's Books

Special thanks to Jan Burchett and Sara Vogler

First published in Great Britain in 2007
by Hodder Children's Books

4

A Catalogue record for this book is available from the British Library

ISBN-13: 978 0 340 93023 6

Typeset in Weiss Antiqua by Avon DataSet Ltd,
Bidford-on-Avon, Warwickshire

Printed and bound in Great Britain by
Clays Ltd, St Ives plc

The paper and board used in this paperback by Hodder Children's Books
are natural recyclable products made from wood grown in
sustainable forests. The manufacturing processes conform to the
environmental regulations of the country of origin.

Hodder Children's Books
A division of Hachette Children's Books
338 Euston Road, London NW1 3BH
An Hachette Livre UK company

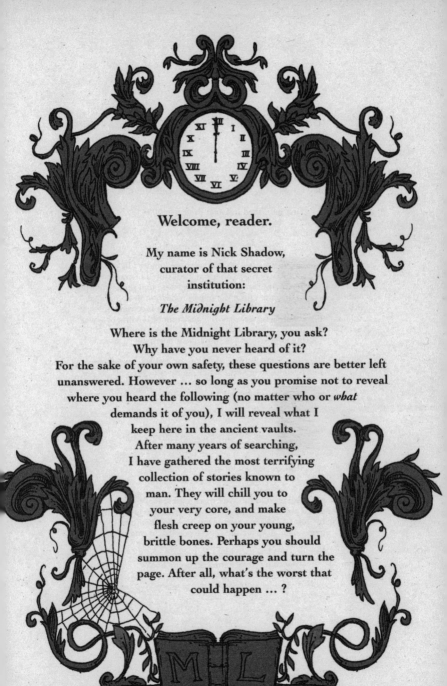

Welcome, reader.

My name is Nick Shadow,
curator of that secret
institution:

The Midnight Library

Where is the Midnight Library, you ask?
Why have you never heard of it?
For the sake of your own safety, these questions are better left
unanswered. However … so long as you promise not to reveal
where you heard the following (no matter who or *what*
demands it of you), I will reveal what I
keep here in the ancient vaults.
After many years of searching,
I have gathered the most terrifying
collection of stories known to
man. They will chill you to
your very core, and make
flesh creep on your young,
brittle bones. Perhaps you should
summon up the courage and turn the
page. After all, what's the worst that
could happen … ?

The Midnight Library: Volume IX

Stories by Jan Burchett and Sara Vogler

CONTENTS

THE WHISPERER

Rachael stared at the school notice-board. She couldn't believe her luck! There it was, in big bubble capitals – 'JOURNALISTS WANTED!' Rachael could feel her heartbeat quicken as she stepped up close to read the small print. The students were going to start their own newspaper, called *Free Speech*, and they needed people to write articles for it. What could be better? It was just up her street. Rachael was determined to become a journalist – so determined that she'd been working really hard for the past year to get decent enough grades to go to college.

'Hi, Rachael! What are you looking at?' Her best friend Amy came up and draped a casual arm round Rachael's shoulders.

Rachael nodded towards the notice. Amy read it quickly. 'I'm going to put my name down,' Rachel told her. 'Think how great that would look on my application form for college if I wrote for the school paper.'

Amy wrinkled up her nose. 'I don't know why you want to do journalism,' she said. 'You're too nice. You'd have to pester soap stars about their love lives, and interview parents when their kids have just been killed. It's not you at all.'

'I won't be doing any of that,' said Rachael. 'I'm going to write about saving starving children and peace efforts in war zones and the destruction of the rainforest. Rachael Worthy – foreign correspondent.' It sounded good, she thought, smiling to herself.

An eager Year 7 barged in front of them to sign up for trampoline club. As soon as he'd gone Rachael and Amy read the rest of the notice.

If you're interested, put your name below and give me an idea of what sort of article you want to write. Email copy to me by next Monday morning. If it's late it won't go in. EmmaHammett@Freespeech.net

Underneath was a long list of people and all the things they were going to write about. Rachael's heart sank. She would never have imagined that so many students would be interested. How could she ever compete with them? OK, there were some that probably wouldn't make it into print. Daisy Blunt wanted to write about her pet gerbil, Sweetums, and Christopher Rockingham seemed to have been inspired by a trip to 'Barometer

World'. But then there were the others further down the list. And they sounded fantastic. Georgina Fearon had encountered a shark off Bondi Beach, and Brennan Morley would be writing about his trial for the National Youth Tennis Academy.

Rachael's excitement evaporated.

'Maybe I won't bother,' she said. 'I wouldn't be able to think of anything half as good as that.'

'Don't do yourself down!' said Amy. 'You know you're great at English. I wish I could write like you.'

But Rachael was having second thoughts. Even if she did submit something for the paper, it wouldn't be easy to get it to Emma. Rachael had no computer, let alone access to the internet. Everyone she knew had at least one computer and most of her friends and classmates had their own laptops. But her dad staunchly refused to even think about buying one. Whenever she pleaded with him he would launch into his usual speech.

'Computers are not healthy for you, Rachael. All you'll do is sit up in your bedroom surfing the net or playing games. We'll never see you again!'

'He is such a dinosaur!' Rachael muttered under her breath.

Angela Upson walked past with her friends.

'Hey, what's this?' she said, stopping by the notice-board and peering at the *Free Speech* poster. 'Great, I'm up for that!' and she pushed past Rachael to put her name down. She strolled away, laughing and chatting with her group. Angela was one of the most popular girls in the school, petite and pretty, with blonde hair that always shone. And on top of it all, she seemed really nice. Rachael would have loved to have been like her, one of the A list. But Rachael knew that girls like Angela wouldn't want to be seen with a no-hoper like her.

'What I would give to be part of that group,' said Rachael wistfully.

'Let's face it, Rach,' sighed Amy. 'We'll never be cool enough.'

Rachael always tried to look cool – she had highlights in her hair and always tried to wear trendy stuff. But she didn't really have the confidence to pull it off. She peered at what Angela had written on the list. *When I went backstage at the Pop Awards*. That would definitely get in. No doubt about it.

They watched as Angela and her friends reached the end of the corridor. Angela peeled away from the others and went to cuddle up to Will Cain, her boyfriend. Some people had all the luck. Not only was Angela pretty and popular, she also was going out with Will, hero of the school football team. And Will was such a dream: tall with spiky hair and not a spot in sight. Only Angela could land someone that gorgeous!

Rachael sighed. What was she thinking? She had no hope of getting published with people like Angela around.

'So you're not going to put your name down? Yeah, well – probably for the best,' teased Amy.

Rachael was about to agree when she felt a little worm of rebellion squiggle inside her. She would never be a journalist if she gave up at the first hurdle. She would write for *Free Speech* and what's more it would be a fantastic piece. Everyone would be talking about her and her writing.

'Oh yes I am,' said Rachael defiantly. 'Just watch me!'

She put her name down on the list before she changed her mind. But she left the subject blank.

All week, Rachael racked her brains to come up with a brilliant idea for an article. It was going to have to be the best idea ever to get published.

'Right,' she said to herself. *'Funky Fashion*. That sounds good.'

She scribbled it down on a piece of paper. No, she thought, she would have to do lots of research for that and she didn't have time. *My Best Read*, she wrote next. That should be easy. She loved reading.

'No good,' she said to her reflection in her dressing-table mirror. 'It's not exactly cool.'

Then she had another idea. *Top Ten Greatest Films Ever*, she wrote in big bold letters. Then she crossed it out.

'Someone else will probably think of that,' she muttered.

By Sunday, she still hadn't come up with anything. She sat in her room staring at her notepad. But gazing at an empty page wasn't getting her anywhere. She picked up her pen. *How to impress a teenage audience*, she wrote in big letters. She stared at it again but still nothing came to mind. And time was running out. All copy had to be with Emma Hammett, the paper's editor, by tomorrow morning. Rachael hated to admit it, but maybe she wasn't cut out to be a journalist after all. Surely a real journalist would have ideas pouring out of her head!

This was hopeless. She was thinking too hard

about it. She needed to forget it for a while. Grabbing her mobile, she rang Amy.

'I'm going nuts here,' she told her. 'Can I come round to yours?'

'Course,' said Amy. 'But I've just promised to go to the supermarket for some milk. Meet me in the high street and then we can walk back to mine after.'

When they met at the supermarket, there was a long queue at the cash desk. At last they burst out of the shop door. Amy was clutching the milk and a movie magazine she'd bought.

'I thought I'd get the giggles,' said Rachael, 'when that old man paid for his shopping all in pennies.'

'Especially when the assistant dropped half of them!' shrieked Amy.

Arm in arm, they set off towards Amy's house. Rachael would just stop for a coffee, and then she'd go home – hoping that inspiration was waiting for her there.

But as they took the short cut through the park,

Rachael saw that there was someone ahead, leaning against a tree. It was Will Cain and he had Angela in his arms. He leaned forward and the two of them kissed. *Lucky Angela*, she thought. She'd love to have a boyfriend, especially one like Will.

But suddenly Will pulled his head back and Rachael got a good look at the girl in his arms. *Oh my God!* It was Gemma Brown from the year below. With a smile, she reached up and pulled Will's face back down to hers. Will Cain was cheating on Angela Upson. This was awful!

'Amy!' she gasped. And then stopped. She loved Amy to bits but there was one thing Amy couldn't do and that was keep a secret. And this had to be kept secret. If Amy got wind of it the whole school would know every detail by first break tomorrow. And then Angela would be sure to hear of it. Rachael curled up inside when she thought of how awful Angela would feel. They had to go back the other way – and now!

'Yeah?' asked Amy vaguely. She had started

reading her magazine as the two of them walked along.

Rachael spun Amy round so fast that her friend nearly fell over.

'What's going on?' demanded Amy, looking up. 'What are you doing?'

'Er . . . shakes!' spluttered Rachael, grabbing her friend by the arm and marching her back towards the shops. 'I suddenly fancy a shake. Come on, let's go back to the high street. My treat.'

'You don't have to push me there, you know,' complained Amy. 'I'm always on for a shake.'

'Sorry,' giggled Rachael. 'My enthusiasm got the better of me.' She waved her hands dramatically in the air. 'I heard the call of Simply Shakes and couldn't resist!'

'I understand that,' nodded Amy. 'Last time I had a chocolate and banana one and I thought I'd gone to heaven!'

It was only when they were safely inside Simply

Shakes that Rachael breathed a sigh of relief. Now Amy need never know what she'd seen. Rachael loved her best friend – but there were some things it was best not to tell her. Amy didn't mean to blab, she just couldn't help herself.

They got their shakes and found a table near the window.

Amy slurped some of her shake. 'This peach and walnut surprise is fab,' she sighed.

Rachael sipped her orange sherbet without even tasting it.

'Great,' she agreed. But she wasn't really listening. She couldn't believe Will Cain. What was he thinking of, to cheat on Angela Upson? What a worm! He needed someone to put him straight. It certainly wasn't going to be her, though. She was far too shy.

And then an idea hit her so hard she nearly swallowed her straw. There was a way she could put him straight! In an article for the paper! She would write a column about real-life issues that affected kids. And where better to start than with betrayal? She wouldn't mention any names – that wouldn't be fair on Angela or Will. But she could talk about cheating in general. With any luck Will would read it and see the error of his ways.

Rachael gulped down the rest of her shake. She wanted to get home as soon as possible. She had an article to write!

'Amy, I've got to go,' she said, pushing her glass away and standing up.

'What? But I thought you were coming back to mine?'

'I know, I'm sorry,' said Rachael, grabbing her bag. 'I've got an article . . . I mean . . . I've suddenly remembered I have an English essay to write.' She didn't dare tell Amy about her idea.

'Rachael, wait!' shouted Amy.

'Er, see you,' called Rachael as she ran out of the door.

* * *

'You're the coolest student in school. You've got it all. Everyone thinks you're fantastic. But beware! It could all go to your head . . .' Rachael was reading over what she'd written. It was looking pretty good – even if she did say so herself.

She was beginning to think that her words could help more people than just Will. She could really do some good. Who knew who might read this and change their mind about cheating? She'd be saving loads of couples from sorrow. Surely this had a chance of getting in the school paper!

'It's a recipe for heartache,' she carried on. She was pleased with that bit. To think she had sat up here in her bedroom earlier and not known what to write.

Inspired, she scribbled away until she had the content of the article exactly as she wanted it.

She leaned back on her pillows and sucked her pen. This didn't have to stop here. Next week she'd write about something else. It wouldn't be hard to find a subject now that she had her focus. Kids of her age often had difficult stuff going on in their lives. They might like to know that someone out there understood and was sympathetic.

Now all she had to do was get her work over to the editor. It had to be emailed and that had to be done tonight. She couldn't ask Amy if she could use her computer. Not after mucking her about earlier. If *only* she had one at home! None of this would be a problem. She snatched up her notebook, grabbed her bag and ran down the stairs. She could see her dad in the kitchen peeling potatoes.

'I'm just going to the internet café in the high street,' Rachael called out, as she opened the front door. 'I've got some work that has to be emailed and as we don't have a computer . . .'

'That's fine, love,' beamed her father. 'Dinner won't be for another hour. And at least you're getting some exercise. If you had your own computer, you'd be sitting in front of it like a pudding. As I always say . . .'

Rachael didn't wait to hear the end of the

sentence. It would be the same as always. She slammed the front door and ran off up the path. She wondered whether to take her bike. It would be quicker, but she didn't want to leave it outside the café. There was nothing to secure it to.

She walked as fast as she could to the high street. The internet café was at the other end. She went past all the closed and shuttered shops. The town was very quiet on Sunday evenings but she knew the café would be open. Cyber Café was open twenty-four/seven. She could see its neon sign.

But when she got there she couldn't believe her bad luck. There were no lights on. The sign in the window said the café was closed for refurbishment! And judging by the bits of wood and pots of paint she could see scattered about in there it certainly didn't look as if it would reopen tonight. What was she going to do? She had this fantastic article in her bag and it was all going to be for nothing if she didn't get it to Emma Hammett this evening.

There was only one thing to do. She had to find

another internet café. Surely there must be another one in the town. New places were always springing up. It was beginning to get dark but she had her mobile with her so she felt perfectly safe. But she'd lay it on thick when she got home. She'd tell her father she'd walked miles on her own to find somewhere to send a simple email. Then maybe he'd buy her a computer.

She went back down the high street and along all the other shop-lined roads that fed into it. No internet cafés anywhere. Just when she thought she was going to have to give up she came to a narrow turning that she didn't remember ever going down. She was about to pass by when she caught sight of a faded sign pointing down the alleyway. It read: 'Internet Café'!

She stepped into the street. It was gloomy, with tall buildings on either side. There were some shops here and there but they didn't look as if they'd been open for years. The rubbish bins were overflowing and the pavement was wet and slimy.

Rachael shivered as a strong gust of cold wind hit her in the face. She pulled her jacket more tightly around her body. How odd! Where had that come from? It wasn't a windy day. Then she heard a scuttling, scrabbling noise behind her. She swung round nervously. But it was just a crisp packet, blowing along in the gutter towards her. It came to rest against a door that suddenly blew open with a horrible creaking of hinges. There was another sign on the door: 'Internet Café'.

Light spilled out from the opening. Rachael crept forward and peered cautiously inside. To her amazement, the inside of the building was completely different from the dirty, ancient brickwork of the outside. It was warm and bright, bathed in a cosy orange glow. Tidy rows of desks with up-to-the-minute computers were ranged along the walls. She'd found it! Just when she'd been about to give up and go home. It must be fate!

Did she have the nerve to go in? The place was full of young people, all tapping away. They'd be bound to look up and stare at her if she went through the door. It never bothered her when she went to her usual internet café. She knew most of the faces there. And if there were any problems here, no one at home knew where she was. But she told herself she was overreacting. She was fine. She had her mobile with her. She could feel it in her pocket. She took a deep breath and stepped into the café.

A few people did look up as she went towards the main desk. But they didn't seem particularly interested in her. At the counter she asked the man for an hour's slot. That should be enough. She would want to type carefully and maybe do a bit of editing, but her article wasn't that long.

'Sorry,' said the man. 'I haven't got any free terminals and we're closing in half an hour. There's no point waiting.'

He picked up a newspaper and turned to the sports pages. Rachael looked round desperately. Surely someone was going to finish in a minute and free up a terminal! But everyone seemed hard at work. Then she noticed a computer up and running, standing empty in the corner. Why hadn't he directed her to it? It wasn't as if it was invisible. There was a spotlight shining right on the chair.

'What about that one?' she asked the man. 'Over there.' She pointed to the corner.

'Not sure it's working properly,' he grunted. 'It's an old model, due for replacement.'

'Look,' said Rachael urgently, 'I really need to use a computer tonight. Can't I try it?'

The man shrugged. 'OK then. You can have it for half price.'

Rachael scrabbled in her bag for her purse.

'Pay me after,' he said. 'Just in case it doesn't work.'

Rachael raced to the computer. With her deadline tomorrow morning she had to get the article written and emailed tonight or she might as well forget all about writing for the school paper.

Rachael accessed the email account that Amy

had set up for her. There were a few messages from friends in her inbox but she ignored these and clicked 'compose'. She typed in Emma's address. She couldn't wait to get started. She was at a computer, she would get the piece to Emma in time and she was sure that this was something that people were going to want to read. She was hoping to do some good. Someone like Will Cain might read it and change their mind about cheating.

Notebook at her side, Rachael started to type. She never thought she would be so grateful for having done that boring keyboard skills class at school. The teacher had said she had a fast typing speed and tonight her fingers were flying over the keys. It must be because she was so enthusiastic about writing for the paper.

She watched her words as they appeared on the screen. She felt confident and powerful – it felt good. How much better the words looked on screen than in her scrubby handwriting! She didn't need to refer to her notebook at all. The words were just flowing. She felt almost hypnotized by the screen.

Rachael felt a sudden twinge of cramp in one of her hands. She leaned back to stop and give her fingers a rub. But her hands refused to leave the keyboard! They carried on typing. In fact, they were typing faster than ever now and whatever she did she could not pull them away. They seemed to be held there by some strange force. And now the keys were moving before she had even touched them, as if they were predicting her words! What was going on? She stared at the screen. There must be something wrong with her eyes, the words were blurring in front of her. She blinked hard. At last the words came back into focus. She couldn't believe her eyes.

'This is weird,' she muttered. '"Cheating can be cool",' she read.

These weren't her words!

Perhaps she had hit the wrong key somewhere because it seemed that a different file had come up.

22

Someone else's file. But her hands went on typing and the words kept appearing on the screen, line after line. The man was right. There was definitely something wrong with this computer. She dragged her gaze away from the screen and tried to ask her neighbour for help. Against her will, her head snapped back to look at the screen again. She sat rigidly in her chair, arms outstretched in front of her. And all the time her hands kept typing.

She read the words as her fingers feverishly worked away. It was still an article about cheating in love. But it wasn't saying that cheating was wrong. Quite the opposite.

Every sentence told the reader how thrilling it was to deceive your loved one. This wasn't what she wanted to say at all! And now the article was reminding the reader to keep their cheating a secret or take the consequences. It finished by dropping heavy hints about a certain captain of the school football team who was having a fling with someone who was not his steady girlfriend. And he was not as clever as he thought. He'd been seen. The words suddenly changed to capitals.

HE'D BETTER WATCH OUT. SOMETHING UNPLEASANT IS COMING HIS WAY.

This is terrible, thought Rachael. *I can't possibly send it. I wasn't going to drop any hints about Will Cain.* But before she could do anything to stop it her hand jerked to the mouse, the cursor hit 'send' and the email disappeared from the screen.

Immediately, Rachael's hands dropped to her sides. The strange feeling that had possessed her was gone. She found she could move normally again. There was no time to lose. She had to send Emma another email straight away, telling her to ignore the first one. Then she would redo her article, properly this time. Suddenly she was plunged into darkness. The café lights were being turned off.

Rachael looked round and was amazed to find

she was the last one in the café. She hadn't noticed everyone else going. The man was walking along the line of terminals, turning each one off as he went. He arrived at her desk.

'Please,' she gasped. 'Can I have a bit longer? There's something I have to write.'

'I'm closing,' said the man. 'Come back tomorrow.'

'Tomorrow's too late!' insisted Rachael. 'At least let me send one more email – just one. It's really important.'

But the man wouldn't listen. 'Time's up,' he growled. He pushed her hand aside, clicked the mouse and shut the computer down. Then he walked to the front desk and stood there, jangling his keys. There was nothing Rachael could do. Slowly, she walked between the rows of terminals, cursing the stupid computer. 'Hang on a minute,' called the man as she got to the door. 'You haven't paid.'

He held out his hand for the money.

'But that thing didn't work properly,' Rachael protested. 'There's something wrong with it – just like you said. It's got a mind of its own . . . What was there on the screen . . . well, it wasn't mine. It wouldn't write what I wanted . . .'

She tailed off, embarrassed. It all sounded so crazy, as if she was making it up. The man obviously thought so too.

'You didn't seem to be having any trouble,' he told her. 'You're just making excuses. Pay up.'

Rachael had no choice. She put the money on to the counter and left. As she stepped out into the dark night she wondered how on earth she was going to explain to Emma Hammett what had happened.

The moment she arrived at school next morning Rachael made straight for Emma's classroom. The sooner this horrible mistake was cleared up the better. With any luck Emma wouldn't have read her email yet. She'd tell Emma to delete it and ask her for some extra time. After school she'd go straight back to the internet café to type out her real piece.

Emma was sitting with a group of friends. They all looked up as Rachael approached.

'Rachael!' exclaimed Emma. 'Got your email!'

Rachael's heart sank.

'That's why I'm here,' she said. It was awful speaking in front of all Emma's friends. Who knew what she'd told them about her dreadful article! 'I'm so sorry it turned out like that. Please delete it. Forget everything you read. I know it's awful. I'll do it again.'

'No you won't!' said Emma firmly.

Oh, no! Rachael had blown her one chance of writing for the paper. Emma was never going to let her submit anything else. Emma stood up, took her by the arm and led her out of the classroom. At least she wasn't going to humiliate her in front of the whole class.

'You won't change a word, Rachael Worthy,' she told her as she pulled Rachael along the corridor to an empty classroom. 'It was fantastic! Though I must admit I had to look twice at the name when I saw it was yours. To be honest, I'd always had you down as a bit of a goody-goody. Worthy by name and worthy by nature. But not now!'

Rachael realized she was gaping at Emma. Emma liked her article! But it wasn't what she'd meant to write. It was trouble-stirring. And what would people think of her when they saw her name at the bottom?

'It got out of hand,' Rachael told Emma. 'I wanted to say how awful cheating is – not how fun.'

'Keep your voice down!' hissed Emma, looking over her shoulder at the classroom door. 'No one must get a sniff of what's in the paper until they read it on Friday.'

'Please don't publish it,' Rachael pleaded. 'Just let me write it again!'

'Too late,' shrugged Emma. 'I liked it and it's in. I pasted it in last night, the moment I read it. Your article's got pride of place – middle page spread.

Kids want to read pieces like yours, contentious and gossipy. And I want them to read the paper. My school newspaper is going to be the biggest thing ever!'

She grasped Rachael by the arm. The look on Emma's face was fierce. 'And if you want to keep that prime slot you'd better come up with another piece of writing just like that for next week.' She let go of Rachael's arm and smiled. 'Don't you get it? I'm offering you a weekly column.'

Emma turned and began to walk back to her classroom.

Rachael watched her go. A weekly column, she repeated to herself. A weekly column, just like a proper journalist. And someone like Emma Hammett thought she was good! But she kept coming back to the article. She couldn't be associated with such spitefulness, could she?

The article was going to appear on Friday with her name on it. It didn't bear thinking about. She'd never hold her head up again in school. How could she get out of it? She had to think of a way. Then it came to her.

'Emma!' she called, running to catch up with her. She lowered her voice. 'OK, I'll do the column. But I really don't want anyone to know it's me. Can I have a pen name?'

Emma stopped at the door of her classroom. 'That's a brilliant idea!' she grinned. 'That will really add spice to it all. Let's think. What could you be called? . . . I've got it. You are the Whisperer.'

At last it was Friday. Rachael had never been in such a hurry to get to school. She quickly pulled a comb through her hair, rammed her books into her bag and only found halfway to school that she didn't have her mobile with her.

By first break the school was buzzing. The paper had only been out an hour but it looked like everyone had read it. Rachael had a copy in her bag but she hadn't had the nerve to open it. As she queued up in the canteen for a Coke she could hear the students behind her chattering away about it.

'Have you read the middle pages?'

'Yes. Twice. I couldn't believe it!'

'Best bit of the paper!'

'I wonder who the Whisperer is.'

Rachael felt a secret tingle of excitement. Amy came running up to her waving a copy of *Free Speech* in her face.

'This is fantastic!' she exclaimed. 'Best thing that's happened round here for ages!'

'I haven't read it yet,' said Rachael, trying to sound unconcerned.

'What?' Amy shrieked in her ear. 'You haven't read the Whisperer? You must be the only one in the whole school. What have you been doing all morning?'

They got their drinks and sat down. Amy spread out the paper and jabbed her finger at it. Rachael scanned the pages quickly. Emma had done as she'd asked. Her name was not on there. And it did look

31

good. In one corner was the silhouette of a figure with its finger to its lips, with 'The Whisperer' in a wobbly, slightly mysterious font above its head. Underneath was the headline: 'CHEAT OF THE WEEK!'

'It's obvious who this cheat is,' said Amy with relish. 'I wonder if Angela Upson's read it yet. She's not going to be too pleased. If I was Will Cain I'd go into hiding!'

'It's not definitely Will Cain,' protested Rachael feebly. 'It doesn't name him . . . er . . . at least, I'm assuming it doesn't.'

'You're so sweet, Rachael,' laughed Amy. 'You don't want to think badly of anybody, do you? It's got to be Will. Listen to this.' She picked up the paper and began to read out loud. '"The captain of a certain school football team not a million miles away from here" – see, Rachael, I told you it was him – "has been seen with someone who isn't his girlfriend. And they weren't discussing the offside rule!"' She slapped the school newspaper back down on the table. 'If that's not Will Cain then I'm a baboon.'

Rachael suddenly realized she'd better look shocked, or Amy might get suspicious that she knew more of the story than she was letting on.

'I suppose you're right,' she said. 'How terrible! Poor Angela.'

'He's a rat!' agreed Amy. But Amy wasn't bothering to hide the delight on her face at such a juicy bit of gossip. Rachael had been right not to tell her before.

'By the way,' said Amy. 'Did you submit anything in the end? Is it in here?'

'Well,' said Rachael, trying to sound vague. 'If my name's not there . . .'

All through lunch-time she heard people talking about the Whisperer, even a couple of teachers. She couldn't believe that her article had proved so popular. She wondered if Angela had read it. She soon found out in her food technology class. Both

Will and Angela were in her set. It was all quiet. Mrs Bolton ruled her kitchens with a ladle of iron and no one dared chat in her lessons. They had all been designing trifles and today was the day when they put their theories to the test and actually made them.

Rachael was sharing a workstation with Will and Angela. It wouldn't have made any difference if Mrs Bolton did allow talking. Angela was maintaining a frosty silence with Will, and Rachael would never have dared talk to either of them anyway. But it was so uncomfortable. Suddenly Angela started muttering furiously at Will. Rachael looked up from arranging her sponge fingers. Angela had moved to Will's side of the table. Everyone stopped arranging their trifles as she began to shout.

'You are such a cheating lowlife!'

Will tried to grin. 'Come on, Ange,' he said. 'Lighten up. It didn't mean anything. It was just a bit of fun.'

'Fun?' screamed Angela, her face like thunder.

She picked up a jug of cold custard and poured it over his head.

Then she burst into tears and dashed out of the room, slamming the door behind her. It took Mrs Bolton ages to quieten the class down and all the time Will stood like an idiot, dripping custard. As soon as their teacher took him off to clean him up, Amy nudged Rachael.

'The Whisperer got it right,' she giggled. 'Something unpleasant did come his way. I can't think of anything worse than being drenched in cold custard!'

Rachael felt terrible. She had made this happen. Her article had made the most famous couple in school break up. *But wait a minute*, she thought. *It wasn't my article that did the damage. It was that strange computer at the internet café. And Will had been cheating after all.*

'Perhaps I did do some good in the end,' she said to herself as she walked home after school. 'Angela's free from a two-timing rat, and maybe other cheats will think twice about doing the dirty on their partners. I'll just have to be more careful how I write my next piece.'

She didn't want to be the cause of any more scenes like that. And she wasn't going to use that dodgy computer at the internet café again.

She decided to start her next article the moment she got home. She would write it by hand. Then she would go to school very early on Monday and use one of the school computers to send it to Emma.

As soon as Rachael stepped inside the hall her mum called to her from the lounge.

'You had a phone call just now,' she said. 'Someone called Emma Hammett. I wasn't really sure what she was on about, but she said you'd know what she meant.'

'What did she say, then?' asked Rachael, putting her head round the door.

'She said keep up the good work and make sure the next one is even better. What's that all about?'

'Oh, nothing,' answered Rachael. 'Just . . . some homework we were doing together.'

Rachael sat at the kitchen table, her notebook in front of her and pen in hand. Emma needn't worry. The Whisperer wouldn't let her down. Although, if Emma was waiting for her to do another piece like this week's she had another think coming. It was going to be hard coming up with something that wasn't malicious but still interesting. But Rachael was sure she could do it. She'd show Emma that nasty gossip wasn't the only thing kids wanted to read. But what to write? How could she actually top today's article?

After half an hour she was tired of staring at the blank sheet of paper in front of her. She gazed out of the window. No inspiration there. She chewed her pen. It was going to be a long evening!

The sound of the phone ringing broke the silence. She bounded into the hall and grabbed it off the wall.

'Hi, Rachael!' She was glad to hear Amy's voice at the other end. 'What are you doing tonight?'

'Er . . . nothing much,' said Rachael. 'Why?'

'Want to go to the cinema? There's that new Brent Finnan movie on.'

Rachael thought for a moment. It was going to take a lot of pen chewing before she managed to produce anything for *Free Speech*. She ought to stay in. But then she reasoned that she had the whole weekend to think about it. Inspiration was bound to strike before Monday. And she adored Brent Finnan.

'You're on,' she said.

'Good.' Amy sounded pleased. 'Let's meet outside the cinema at seven. And by the way, why aren't you answering your mobile? I rang you a few times earlier then I gave up and decided to use the landline. I was beginning to think you didn't want to speak to me!'

'As if!' laughed Rachael. 'I'm sorry but I never heard it ring. I think I left it under a pile of stuff in my room this morning.'

'Right, then. See you later.'

Rachael put down the phone, ran upstairs and quickly looked for her mobile among the mess on her bedroom floor. She didn't want to go out without it again. But there was no sign of it, even when she'd turned over every scrap of paper and discarded bits of clothing.

Rachael began to worry. Where was her mobile? It wasn't in her bag or her blazer. Had she left it somewhere? She'd better find it before Dad realized she'd lost it. He'd never been keen on the idea of her having one in the first place and would probably annoy her by telling her she was better off without it. 'They're a waste of time and bad for the brain,' was all he would ever say on the subject. *Just like his silly ideas about computers and the internet*, thought Rachael.

The internet café! Maybe she'd left it there! It could easily have dropped out of her pocket – she had left in a bit of a hurry. She'd drop in and ask on the way back from the cinema.

Rachael and Amy arrived in good time for the film and sat in their seats waiting for it to begin. They watched the rest of the audience finding their way to their places with trays of nachos and enormous Cokes. A man clambered past them with a box of popcorn.

'I could murder some of that,' declared Amy, when he'd gone past. 'But I didn't bring enough money out with me.'

Rachael stood up. 'I'll go and get some,' she said. 'We can share a box. We've got ten minutes before the trailers start.'

She made her way out into the foyer, bought the popcorn and was just walking back when she caught sight of Emma Hammett next to the sweet stand. She was about to call out to her but stopped herself. Emma was behaving very strangely. She looked as if she was trying not to be seen. Suddenly her hand shot out, grabbed a bag of mints and slipped it into her pocket. Rachael watched in shock as she made for the door to Screen One.

There was a crowd of lads round the attendant, all holding out their tickets. While the attendant was busy checking them, Emma glanced furtively round, then quickly slipped behind him and through the door. She was sneaking in to the film without a ticket. How could she be so stupid! Rachael was horrified. And what if everyone found out at school? That wouldn't do Emma's reputation any good at all!

Rachael walked slowly back to join Amy. She couldn't get Emma's behaviour out of her head. Emma Hammett didn't know how lucky she was that Rachael had seen her and not Amy. Unlike Amy, Rachael would be able to keep it to herself.

After the film, Rachael remembered that she had to drop in to the internet café and see if her phone was there. But the café was in the opposite direction from her house and she didn't want Amy to know she was going there. If Amy knew she'd been there she was bound to start asking why and

Rachael couldn't possibly tell her about the Whisperer. Amy was full of the film they'd just seen but even so she'd be sure to notice if Rachael set off in completely the wrong direction. So Rachael walked with her the usual way home. Fortunately they would come to Amy's house first. She would double back as soon as Amy had gone in. She managed to answer Amy's chatter but she was relieved when they got to the top of Amy's road.

'Bye,' called Amy. 'I know who I'm going to dream of tonight.' She gave a cheery wave and set off towards her house.

As soon as Amy had shut her front door, Rachael turned and walked quickly back to the narrow street and the internet café. The alley was as dark and decrepit as before. There was no sign of life. Rachael was beginning to wonder whether she'd come to the wrong place. But then the door ahead of her creaked open, just as it had before. She took a deep breath and went inside.

The café was busy again tonight and hardly anyone looked up as she walked past the terminals. When she reached the desk, the man looked up from his paper. He didn't say a word but just reached over to a shelf behind him and produced her mobile phone.

'Thanks,' she said and went back to the door. She'd get off home now. But her eyes flickered back to the old computer she'd used before. No one was using it. The computer seemed to pull her towards it. She threw the money on to the desk and walked over without a word to the man. She sat down, forgetting her decision never to use this terminal again. She was infused with excitement. What better time to start writing the Whisperer's next article? Rachael stretched her hands over the keyboard. Immediately her fingers jerked into a life of their own. They flew over the keys and words she had never thought of appeared on the screen. Just as before, she couldn't take her fingers from the keys or her eyes from the screen. Bewildered, she watched as the article took shape. It was about dishonesty but it went on about a certain character who thought it was a good idea to act like a criminal. A certain character who should know better. With horror Rachael watched the bitchy article forming itself on the screen.

Well, well, well, what a surprise! said the Whisperer. *Who would have thought our school was harbouring a petty thief! Someone who obviously thinks they're invisible when they sneak their way into a film without a ticket – and nick a snack to take in with them! What next?*

WITH E.H. AROUND – LOCK UP YOUR MONEY!

The moment it was finished Rachael's hand jerked over and hit 'send'. She was thrown back, exhausted, in her chair. But now the article was in front of her she no longer felt troubled by what the computer had produced. Instead she had a triumphant smile on her face.

That should do it, she thought. It was a bit spiteful

but it made for good reading. And the end would really hit home!

She wished she could be there to see the look on Emma's face when she read about herself! Rachael had never experienced such power before. It surged through her, making her feel like a different person. This must be how those confident kids at school felt all the time. Her intention of being careful and kind was abandoned. Emma wanted a punchy article. She had got it. And how!

Head held high, Rachael swept through the internet café, out into the street. And stopped dead. She suddenly felt like a balloon that had been popped at the end of a fantastic party. What had she just done? But she couldn't think about it now. She felt as if she was trying to wake up from a really deep sleep. She headed home, trying to shake off the drugged feeling.

By the next morning Rachael had come to her senses. The article last night had been another disaster. Never again! If she was allowed to write any more she would have to type them up on one of the school computers. Or, as a very last resort, she'd ask Amy.

And that was only if Emma forgave her. By Monday morning the Whisperer might be no more.

Emma didn't wait until Monday. Rachael nearly jumped out of her skin as her mobile phone rang at eight o'clock the next morning. Nervously, she answered it. Emma's tone was icy.

'Meet in Cassland Park – NOW! I'll be by the fountain.'

And she hung up without another word.

Rachael threw on some clothes and raced out to the shed where her bike was. She needed to get to the park quickly. She didn't dare keep Emma waiting.

Emma was already at the fountain when Rachael arrived. She was striding up and down. She looked furious. Rachael climbed off her bike and walked slowly to meet her.

'What exactly do you think you're playing at?' Emma shouted at her. 'It wasn't funny and in no way was it subtle. Everyone will know it was me — and it's none of your business anyway. If you think I'm going to print your article you're seriously deluded.'

Rachael wished she could dig a big hole and hide in it.

'I'm sorry,' she gabbled. 'I didn't mean to send . . . I mean . . . I didn't write . . .'

This was hopeless. She knew Emma was right. It was none of her business. But she wouldn't be able to convince Emma of that after sending her such a spiteful piece — a piece that she'd never meant to write in the first place. But Emma wasn't even listening to her feeble excuses.

'I don't want to hear anything more from you,' she snapped.

'So, you don't want any more of my articles?' faltered Rachael.

'You've got one last chance,' hissed Emma. 'If you

can't get a really good article to me by Monday morning I'm pulling the Whisperer column and you won't even be able to do Lost and Found ads for me.'

She stalked off.

Rachael watched her go. She wanted to cry. She should never have written that about Emma.

But there was one ray of hope. She was still on the paper! As long as she could come up with something sensational for Monday, Emma would give her another chance.

She got on her bike and began to cycle slowly home. She came to the crossroads with the high street and slowed down. Then, without any warning, a motorbike suddenly roared towards her. She had no time to swerve. She just caught sight of the faces of the two riders as the bike roared past, catching her front tyre. The next thing she knew she had hit the pavement – hard.

'My God, are you all right?' A shop assistant had come out of the newsagent's nearby and was standing over her. He reached down to pull her up. 'Good job you were wearing a helmet.' He looked down the road in the direction the bike had taken. 'Stupid idiots!'

In a daze Rachael staggered to her feet and inspected herself. She had a gaping hole in her jeans, her knee was bleeding and her hands were grazed and covered in grit. And it hurt! She could see everyone gawping at her. She tried to brush herself down. 'Thank you,' she said feebly. 'I'll be all right now. Better be getting home.'

'Well, if you're sure,' said the assistant. 'I've half a mind to phone the police about this. Do you know who they were?'

'Afraid not,' said Rachael. She began to wheel the bike away. She certainly did know who they were but she wasn't going to tell the shop assistant that. She didn't want to cause any more trouble today. She'd recognized them immediately. It was Ian and Mark Webb, two irritating pranksters from her school.

She limped along the high street, pushing her bike, hoping not too many people were staring at her. She must look a sight. Though that was nothing to how Ian and Mark would look if they had an accident. They had no helmets and no leathers. And, now she came to think of it, neither of them was old enough to ride a motorbike.

She began to feel anger bubbling up. Ian and Mark had knocked her flying and they hadn't cared. She could have been badly hurt. If they didn't kill themselves first they were sure to kill someone else soon. She was suddenly aware of a buzzing sound in her ears and she felt dizzy for a moment. It must be the effects of the fall, she decided. But then her head cleared. It was as if a computer had been switched on inside her brain. She was aware of her heart beating faster. She forgot all about her aches and pains. She felt energized. New and exciting thoughts started whizzing around. She knew exactly what she was going to write in her next article. And she was going to write it now. There was only one place she could do that. The internet café. But she was going in the wrong direction. She turned round, crossed the road and got on her bike, ignoring the soreness in her palms as she gripped the handlebars. She sped off, feet pedalling furiously, back down the high street.

'Just you wait, Ian and Mark Webb,' she muttered through gritted teeth. 'I'm going to make you pay for this.'

There was a pedestrian crossing just before the turning for the café and the lights were red.

'Come on! Come on!' she almost shouted at them. She gripped the handlebars fiercely and got one foot ready to push away as soon as they changed.

'Rachael!' came a cry. She recognized the voice. It was Amy. Amy was coming out of Chicks, their favourite shop, and waving carrier bags at her. 'Come and look. They've got a great bargain rail. I've bought three skirts and a jacket!'

Rachael felt a surge of annoyance at her friend. *I'll never get there at this rate!* she thought.

But just then the lights changed to green and, without a word to her friend, Rachael sped off. Normally she would be happy to spend hours in Chicks, but today she had no time for buying clothes. She had to get to the café. She had to write her article. She had to have revenge.

She skidded to a halt outside the café, threw her bike down on to the pavement and pushed the door open. As usual the café was busy but for once she didn't care if people looked at her. She didn't care how dishevelled she looked. The man behind the desk put his paper down and stared at her appearance for a moment. She just nodded at him, slapped some money on to the counter and marched over to the computer in the corner. As usual, no one else was using it. It was waiting for her.

Rachael took her seat and stretched her hands over the keyboard. A slow smile spread across her face and she felt her heartbeat calm and steady. Amy's puzzled face flashed up for a moment in her head. She'd been really rude to her. But she pushed the memory away. She had a story to write. She was going to wipe the floor with those two stupid boys on the motorbike. She opened an email and tapped in the title.

MOTORBIKE MAYHEM!

It was a brilliant start. In a trance Rachael punched away at the keys. The article quickly took shape, telling everyone about two boys from their school who would remain nameless but who were closely related. 'Despite being well under age they have taken to roaring through the town on a stolen motorbike.' This might not be quite true but never mind. The bike probably belonged to their older brother and she was willing to bet they hadn't asked his permission. So technically it was stolen. Anyway, who cared? It made a better story.

The words swept across the screen. Rachael wondered why she had ever been frightened by what this computer had made her do. The article was turning out exactly how she wanted it. It was really going to hit home.

Especially the bit about how the two brothers had nearly killed someone with their reckless behaviour. Anyone who didn't recognize Ian and Mark Webb from her description must have been walking around school with their eyes closed for the last year.

She was beginning to love this computer and how it gave her the opportunity to write such fantastic articles. She remembered the readers snatching up *Free Speech* the instant it came out and all to read her column! She wanted it to carry on. Her hands flew over the keys.

I predict their reign of terror will end soon, the article finished. *By the time you read this they could well be having a ride in a very different sort of vehicle —*

ONE WITH A BLUE FLASHING LIGHT!

Rachael sat back. Her head was pounding and her hands were tense and cramped. But it was worth it for the feeling of power the computer gave her. This wonderful machine had said just what she wanted. And better than she could have done herself. With a grimace of pain she straightened her fingers and gently stroked the keys. Her and the computer – what a team!

Monday morning was the best start to a school week Rachael had ever had. Emma insisted on sitting next to her in German and went on about how fantastic her article had been.

'Don't ever stop writing,' she whispered, while their teacher was correcting somebody's work on the other side of the classroom. 'Your articles are the best thing about the paper. I reckon you've got a real future in journalism. I'm going to ask the office if we can have extra copies printed this time

– everyone's going to want one.' Emma seemed to have forgotten that only two days ago she'd been furious with her. 'Look, I'm having a party soon. You'll be there, won't you?'

Rachael nodded. 'Course I will,' she said. Emma Hammett thought of her as a friend! Naturally she would – Rachael was her star reporter after all.

As she made her way to her science lesson she bumped into Amy.

'What was up with you on Saturday?' Amy was smiling but she sounded puzzled, and a bit hurt. 'Didn't you see me outside Chicks? I called out to you but you totally ignored me.'

'Saturday?' said Rachael. 'Sorry, Amy. I never saw you . . . I was in a bit of a daze. I'd fallen off my bike and had to get home.' She was telling the truth about the fall at least.

'You were in a right state,' agreed Amy. Then she looked hard at her. 'Hang on a minute. If you were going home you were going the wrong way.'

'Oh . . . well . . . that's because . . .' Rachael was

floundering for an excuse and Amy could see it.

'Something's up,' she said, frowning. 'What is it? You can tell me.'

'No, nothing . . . it's just that . . . I bumped my head when I fell,' Rachael said in a rush, 'and then I set off in the wrong direction. Took me ages to get home,' she finished lamely.

Amy didn't ask any more, but Rachael knew she wasn't convinced. She seemed a bit cool for the rest of the day. Rachael shrugged it off. Amy would get over it.

Rachael couldn't wait to see her article in print but the week seemed to drag by. At last it was Friday. She hurried to school determined to be the first one to pick up a copy of *Free Speech*. Emma had said it would be there before registration.

As she turned down Cowper Crescent she was surprised to see a couple of police cars outside one of the houses. It looked like someone was in trouble. *Good*, thought Rachael. There might be things going on here that would give her the Whisperer's next article. She crossed the road to get a closer look.

Then she stopped. It was the Webbs' house and Ian and Mark were at the door being led out by a couple of policemen. They both looked very pale and scared. Their mum was following them, clutching a coat. She was crying. Ian looked over and saw Rachael. He quickly hid his face in his hands. The boys were bundled into the back of one of the cars and their mum got into the other one. The cars roared off.

Rachael hurried on, a smile playing on her lips. She'd already covered that story. And now those boys had got what they deserved. She was desperate to see how her piece would go down now.

When she got to the school office she couldn't get anywhere near the table where the *Free Speech* was piled up. There were crowds of kids jostling each other and everyone was turning to the middle pages.

'There's only one family that fits that description,' someone was saying.

'It's got to be the Webbs.'

'Have they seen this? There's going to be trouble when they do.'

Suddenly there was a commotion at the main door. A boy from the year below Rachael came bursting in.

'You'll never guess what!' he called to a group of his friends. 'Ian and Mark Webb have been arrested! This morning. I've just seen them go by in a police car. They looked really sick.'

Everyone started talking at once.

'But that's just what the Whisperer said would happen!'

'How did he know?'

'Perhaps he was the one who dobbed them in to the police!'

Rachael felt a thrill at her secret identity. There

was no way anyone would suspect the Whisperer was her. Especially as some of them thought she was a boy! She finally jostled her way to the front and snatched a copy of the paper. She didn't need to read it, of course, but she thought she'd better pretend to. It would look funny if she didn't. Amy suddenly appeared at her side.

'I've been looking for you everywhere!' she exclaimed. 'Have you read it? Whoever the Whisperer is predicted that Ian and Mark Webb would be arrested! Creepy or what!'

Rachael felt a thrill go through her. This was what it must be like to be a real journalist! Your words affected people. They made people talk. It felt great! One thing was certain. She was famous – or, at least, the Whisperer was. Wouldn't people be surprised if they knew that it was Rachael Worthy?

She got a note from Emma at breaktime. 'Great stuff. Who's your source? I suppose that's a trade secret. Anyway, keep them coming!'

Rachael felt wonderful.

It wasn't long before everyone in the school had heard about the fate of Ian and Mark Webb.

Rachael heard all about it as she made her way to maths after first break. Everyone was talking about it and the rumour-mongers had been hard at work.

'They've been arrested,' one boy was announcing. 'And taken to prison!'

'No they haven't,' scoffed his friend. 'They're back at home. But they are going to be charged with under-age and dangerous driving.'

'We won't be seeing them on the motorbike for a while, then,' said the first. 'Not even the Webb brothers would risk that.'

Rachael walked on. Two girls from the netball team were pinning fixture lists on the main board. Their heads were close together. Rachael stopped and pretended to be reading one of the other announcements.

'How did the police get them?' asked the netball captain. She kept her voice low and Rachael had to strain to hear it.

'Caught them redhanded apparently,' her friend told her in the same hushed tone. 'We won't see them in school for a bit. I'm not sorry. They're terrors, those two.'

'Hmm,' agreed the netball captain. 'Weird, though, how the Whisperer predicted it.'

'I can't wait to read next week's. Perhaps we should write in and ask him to guess the lottery numbers!'

Rachael walked off. She was glowing with pride. She couldn't believe that no one could see it beaming off her.

After school Rachael grabbed her bag and set off for the internet café. She didn't even think to let Amy know she wouldn't be walking home with her. She just had to get there. It didn't matter that she had the whole weekend to do her next article. It didn't matter that she had no idea what to write about. Rachael was sure that when she sat down at 'her' computer, she would produce something sensational. As she got closer to the café the buzzing in her ears began and her heart started to race. She welcomed the feeling now. She had a column to write.

She stepped boldly into the internet café and looked over at her computer. But the screen was blank. The computer wasn't on! Had it finally broken down? She looked round for the manager but couldn't see him anywhere. What was she going to do? She'd be lost without this computer. Rachael could feel herself sweating in panic. She thought she was going to cry. Just at that moment, the manager emerged from a back room carrying a box of cups for the drinks machine.

'That . . . terminal in the corner . . .' Rachael could hardly get the words out. 'Is it working?'

The manager sighed, put the box of cups down on the floor and ambled over to the computer. He pressed a button. Rachael felt almost hysterical with relief as it sprang into life.

She sat down. Just like before, the moment she

stretched her hands over the keys the buzzing in her ears stopped and her heart began to beat normally again. She had come home.

She opened a new email and sat back, leaving her hands resting lightly on the keyboard. At first nothing happened. But then she was suddenly jerked forward. Words burst on to the screen as her fingers stabbed at each letter, more furiously than ever before. The tantalizing headline appeared.

BREAKING NEWS!

The school gymnastics team are heading for a fall, the article began. Rachael's eyes were glued to the screen. She knew that the team were going to give a display to the whole school this Friday. The posters had been up for weeks. They were practising for a county competition. But something was going to happen. Something nasty. Fascinated, her fingers moved across the keyboard like an automaton and her lips moved silently as she mouthed the words before her.

The team might be good enough for a county win, but are they being overworked? The Whisperer agrees that competition is good – unless it takes over your life. Certain team members need to be careful. If they allow themselves to be pushed too hard, one of them could have a nasty injury – and that will be the end of any hope for a gymnastic career for them. The athletes are only human, after all, whatever Miss G might think.

Rachael nodded. She too had suffered at the hands of Miss Grimshaw. Her hands typed on and on. This was the best piece the Whisperer had ever done. It would really show what everyone thought of old Grimbags.

And be sure, Miss G will drop any injured gymnast like a shot. We all know how she drives the competitors, too. But do we know why? A little bird has told the Whisperer that Miss G never even got picked for her school team, however much she practised. She couldn't have it then so she is determined to have the glory now no matter what the cost.

AND BEWARE! THAT COST
MAY BE TOO GREAT!

Click! The 'send' button was activated and Rachael's fingers came to a halt. She felt a sudden pang of loss. If only this experience could go on and on. She loved being the Whisperer. To think she'd wanted to write a do-gooder's column!

It looked like next Friday was going to be an interesting day.

Rachael was still on a high when she got to school on Friday. Every time she thought of her article she felt power surge through her. She was the Whisperer and people listened to her. And today she was going to slam Miss Grimshaw with the truth!

In the entrance hall Emma was sticking a hastily written note on the notice-board: *'Free Speech delayed till lunch-time'*. She was fuming!

'Would you believe it!' she ranted, when she saw

Rachael. 'The office hasn't printed them yet because Miss Grimshaw insisted they do a programme for this stupid gymnastic display first. They've promised to have them done by lunchtime. They'd better!' Then she grinned and lowered her voice. 'I can't wait to see old Grimbags' face when she reads your article.'

Nor can I, thought Rachael. *Serve her right.*

She saw Amy further down the entrance hall and ran to meet her.

They linked arms and went into the gym and found some seats with a good view. The gymnastic team were warming up under the barked commands of Miss Grimshaw. There were landing mats making a display floor and, to one side, asymmetric bars had been set up.

'Listen to old Grimbags,' giggled Amy. 'Didn't her mum ever tell her to use please and thank you? She's such a dragon, I'd love to see her cut down to size.'

Rachael just smiled and nodded. She was

bursting to tell Amy that Miss Grimshaw might be in for a bit of a surprise, but she couldn't blow her cover as the Whisperer.

The display began with Miss Grimshaw giving a speech. It went on for ages.

'. . . and I have devoted all my spare time to this team. It is because of me that they are where they are. I never dreamed, when I was a teenage gymnastics star myself, that one day . . .' Miss Grimshaw droned on and on, telling the school how wonderful she was. Rachael stopped listening and pictured the gym teacher's face when she read *Free Speech*.

At last music started and the gymnasts began a team display of cartwheels, back flips, handstands, splits and arabesques – all in time to the rhythm. It was fantastic. Even Rachael had to admit, this team really did deserve to get to the county level.

Then Isabel Townsend stepped forward. She was the star of the team and had just been picked for the national squad. She stood calmly waiting while Miss Grimshaw made an announcement.

'Isabel is going to perform on the asymmetric bars,' she informed everyone triumphantly. 'Please note the full turn in the release, re-grasp movement. And, for the first time, she is also going to attempt a twisting double somersault dismount.'

A look of panic crossed Isabel's face. This was obviously news to her. She muttered something to Miss Grimshaw. 'Of course you're going to do it,' Rachael heard the gym coach snap back. 'Don't disappoint me after all I've done for you!'

Rachael suddenly felt as if she was in a plummeting lift. Her head swam and her stomach lurched. She thought she was going to be sick. The feeling of power drained out of her.

The old Rachael began to surface.

Why had she gone back to use that computer yet again? She should have fought against it. She was disgusted to think how it had taken her over. Never again. But that wasn't going to help now.

Something horrible was going to happen. The Whisperer had predicted it and the Whisperer was always right.

But old Grimbags would never listen to her if she tried to stop the display. There was nothing she could do but watch.

'Are you OK, Rachael?' whispered Amy, pulling at her arm. 'You don't seem to be able to keep still.'

'Er . . . just excited to be watching Isabel,' Rachael hissed back. 'Sorry.'

Isabel had given up protesting to Miss Grimshaw. For a moment she looked defeated, but then she flung her arms in the air and arched her back ready to start. She stepped forwards to the asymmetric bars. She jumped and grasped the lower one, swinging herself up and over it to gain momentum. Her legs were perfectly straight and together the whole time. Isabel knew what she was doing. She was in complete control. Rachael felt herself relax a little. It was going to be OK. Wasn't it?

Isabel flipped to the higher bar and made several rotations, twisting and releasing and catching the bar again and then balancing at the top in a handstand. The audience whooped and clapped wildly as she went through her well-rehearsed routine. Then she began to swing round the bar, faster and faster.

'This must be the famous dismount,' whispered Amy, giving Rachael a nudge.

Rachael felt cold all over. She could hardly bear to watch. *Please let the Whisperer be wrong*, she wished fervently.

Isabel launched herself off the top bar. She started to tuck up for the first somersault. But suddenly her body was twisting out of control, limbs flailing in the air. There were gasps of horror from the audience. For one terrible moment it looked as if she would hit the ground head first. But at the last minute she managed a desperate jerk and righted herself. She hit the mat hard and, with a sickening crack, one leg buckled under her. Isabel collapsed, shrieking in pain, her leg stuck out at an impossible angle.

Miss Grimshaw marched over to her. 'Come on, Isabel,' she roared. 'It's not that bad!' She reached down to pull her up.

'No!' shouted Rachael, leaping to her feet. 'Leave her alone!' The words of all her articles flashed in front of her eyes. She thought of Will Cain and the Webb brothers. They'd been punished because of the Whisperer. And now it was poor Isabel, who hadn't done anyone any harm. Where was it going to end?

Amy pulled her back down on to her seat, giving her a strange look.

'Sorry,' Rachael whispered. 'It's just . . . it's just that I can see Isabel is really hurt.'

Miss Grimshaw glared at Rachael. The head teacher rose from her seat and hurried over to Isabel, who was now writhing in agony on the mat.

'Call an ambulance!' she ordered sharply. 'Everyone get back to your classes.'

Rachael bit her lip. She wished she was a million miles away. She certainly didn't want to be at school any more. Not with *Free Speech* about to come out with the Whisperer's article that predicted all that had just happened.

The audience filed out. Someone pulled at Rachael's sleeve.

Rachael turned. It was Emma, looking at her with a mixture of admiration and horror. 'How did you know?' she hissed.

The school was in shock for the rest of the morning. News spread that Isabel's leg was so badly broken that she would be in traction for weeks. She wouldn't be able to take up her place in the national squad. It was even feared that she might never do gymnastics again.

Rachael was near to despair. She barely heard a word of her geography lesson. How could she . . . or rather, how could the Whisperer have known what was going to happen? And things would only get worse when everyone read the paper. She supposed it was just possible that the office hadn't printed it yet. The moment that morning's lessons were over she'd go and find out. Perhaps she could stop it.

But when she got to the entrance hall at lunch-time she found she was too late. She stood dumbly watching as student after student took a copy and opened it – and turned straight to the middle pages. Soon there were crowds of kids gathered round.

'Oh my God!' exclaimed someone. 'The Whisperer's written all about the display. He's predicted Isabel's accident.'

'That's really weird!'

'Do you think the Whisperer can see into the future?'

Students were starting to look nervously round.

'Don't be stupid,' said a boy, folding up the paper and tossing it in the bin. 'No one can see into the future. Whoever it is has probably just written it. That must be why it was delayed today.'

'That's so sick!'

Rachael wanted to butt in and tell them that the Whisperer hadn't meant any harm. But she knew she couldn't. They wouldn't believe her anyway. She walked off, shaken to the core. This had really got out of control.

She fretted all afternoon, barely hearing what was going on in her lessons. Writing for *Free Speech* wasn't supposed to have been like this. She'd just wanted to write a column which would help people. And that's what she would have done. But the moment she'd sat down at that computer everything had changed. She was hurting everyone around her.

By the time she got home she'd made a big decision. She'd put everything right. She'd stop writing for the school newspaper. Then whatever creepy thing was happening would be over. Everything could go back to normal. That computer at the internet café would just seem like a bad dream.

She grabbed her mobile and called Emma's number.

'It's Rachael,' she said the moment the phone was answered. 'Look, I don't—'

'Rachael!' Emma burst in before she could finish. 'I've had so much grief today because of your article. People don't like it. I've had angry kids breathing down my neck all day – not to mention the teachers. I don't care what you say. The Whisperer has got to go.'

'But that's why I phoned,' said Rachael. 'I don't want to be the Whisperer any more.'

'Well, that suits both of us, then,' snapped Emma. 'You haven't done me any favours, Rachael Worthy. If this paper fails it will all be your fault. You've certainly jinxed Fridays with your stupid column. That's what everyone's saying. I'm going to have to delay the next issue until Monday week. And I'm putting an end to the Whisperer.'

There was a click as Emma rang off.

Rachael couldn't believe the feeling of relief that flooded through her. It was all over.

She immediately rang Amy.

'Can you come round?' she asked. 'I'm sorry I've hardly seen you lately. I'll get some pizzas and we can just hang out together. We haven't done that for ages. It's my fault. I've been a bit tied up with . . . schoolwork.'

'Just try and stop me,' said Amy eagerly. 'I'll bring my new CD. We can listen to it.'

Everything was back to normal – if anything it was better. She got her highest mark ever for an English essay – and every word was her own, written at her own speed. Amy had completely forgotten any problems they'd had. And best of all, on Saturday morning Dad suddenly put a leaflet down in front of her at the breakfast table.

'Look at this,' he grinned. 'I thought you might be interested.'

Rachael quickly scanned the leaflet. 'RUXONS

BIG SALE!' it said in big orange type that almost hurt her eyes. 'Desktops, laptops, and all computer accessories at huge discounts.' She caught her breath.

'I've been thinking,' Dad went on. 'Perhaps it's not such a good idea for you to have to go off in search of a computer every time you've got homework. Shall we go and see if we can get you one of your own? As long as you promise not to spend hours doing that surfing thing.'

Rachael jumped up and flung her arms round his neck. How different her life was going to be! Homework would be a doddle. She could email all her friends without having to rely on Amy. And best of all – no more visits to internet cafés.

There was only one little thing that nagged at the back of Rachael's mind: she was going to miss the buzz of being a proper journalist – the secret thrill of going into school knowing that her column would be the one everybody was talking about. She felt a small pang of regret. But she certainly wouldn't miss the trouble it had caused. She was free of all that.

It still felt strange going into school on Friday morning, knowing that *Free Speech* would be there for everyone to pick up and there would be no Whisperer's column for people to turn to. Rachael had meant to walk straight past the crowd of kids at the table without picking up a copy but something stopped her. Something was different. OK, she'd expected that now the Whisperer's column was finished, there wouldn't be much to get excited about. But she hadn't expected anyone to be upset about it! The readers seemed stunned by what was in front of their eyes. What were they reading? They all had *Free Speech* open at the middle pages. Emma must have put something there in the Whisperer's place. Something amazing!

Amy saw her and thrust a copy at her. 'Have you read this?' she gasped.

Rachael grabbed the middle pages and quickly flicked to the centre of the paper.

What! She blinked hard. It was still there. The Whisperer's column with its familiar silhouette of a figure with its finger to its lips. But Emma had told her that she was going to put an end to the Whisperer. Had she just got rid of Rachael in order to put one of her friends in her place – or even write the columns herself? Rachael was furious.

She straightened the paper angrily and began to read. It was a very short piece, presumably written by Emma. It just told with great regret that this was the last time the Whisperer's column would appear in *Free Speech*. Then there was a paragraph praising the secret work of the columnist. Rachael felt slightly appeased. At least Emma was being generous.

But then she read the last line. It was in capitals.

THE END OF THIS GREAT COLUMN IS DUE TO THE TRAGIC DEATH OF THE WHISPERER IN A CAR ACCIDENT.

Horrified, she dropped the paper and had to scrabble about on the floor picking up the sheets.

'I know,' said Amy, 'it's awful. Do you think it's really true?'

Rachael's shock had now turned to anger. Without answering Amy, she stuffed the copy of *Free Speech* in her bag and made for Emma's classroom.

She heard Amy calling down the corridor after her. 'Rachael! What's up? Where are you going?'

Rachael took no notice and marched straight on. She was going to find Emma Hammett right now and have it out with her. Emma was getting her own back on Rachael – in the cruellest way possible. And Rachael was not going to let her get away with it. But as she got to the door of Emma's room the bell rang for registration. She looked in through the glass. Perhaps she still had time. After all, this was important. But Emma's teacher was already there. Rachael would have to wait till later.

Rachael seethed all morning. Emma had to be told just how hurtful she was being. But it wasn't until lunch-time that Rachael finally spotted her. She just caught a glimpse of Emma as she left the school grounds. Rachael grabbed her bag and sprinted for the gates. She could see Emma up ahead, strolling along with some friends. They turned to cross the road.

'Emma!' Rachael yelled. 'Emma, wait! This is important!'

Emma turned. She looked very surprised to see Rachael belting towards her.

'Er . . . I'll be along in a moment,' she told the girls with her. Her friends crossed the road. Emma waited, tapping her foot impatiently.

As Rachael ran up to her Emma opened her mouth to speak but Rachael didn't give her the chance. She had stewed about this all morning. Emma had gone too far.

'I suppose you think that was funny, don't you!' she demanded, thrusting the crumpled middle section of *Free Speech* at her. 'Well, it wasn't. It was plain sick!'

'I agree,' said Emma, taken aback. 'But your stuff had got so dark recently I just thought it was some black joke of yours. Going out with a bang! Though I don't know why you bothered. No one knows who the Whisperer is, do they?'

Rachael stared at her, hardly taking in what she was saying. 'I don't understand,' she said at last. 'You think I wrote it? But I didn't. I didn't send you any copy. I haven't been near a computer all week.'

Emma shrugged. 'If you say so,' she said, sounding bored. 'But you might like to check your sent emails. I only opened it because it had your name on it. Perhaps someone else thought it would be funny. Who cares anyway? There's no harm done. No one has really died, have they?'

She crossed to join her friends who were waiting for her by the burger bar on the other side of the busy road.

Rachael was consumed with anger. Emma had

made a really sick joke at her expense and now she had the nerve to shrug it off as if it didn't matter! She didn't even have the decency to own up to what she'd done. No way was Rachael going to let that go! She was going to tell Emma exactly what she thought of her. How dare she treat her like that! Hardly noticing the busy traffic whizzing past, Rachael watched Emma on the other side of the road. Emma was chatting and laughing with her friends as if she didn't have a care in the world. Blinded by her anger, Rachael stepped off the pavement towards her.

BANG!

Rachael felt everything move in slow motion as she was flung high into the air. Then she crashed down heavily on to the bonnet of a car. For a split second, she caught sight of the terrified eyes of the driver before she thudded against the hard tarmac of the road.

She lay there motionless for a moment. At first she felt nothing, then pain burst over her. She struggled to open her eyes. There was something wet and sticky around her face and her heart was thumping fast, too fast, in her ears. She closed her eyes again.

Her heart fluttered weakly and everything went dark.

A haze of terrified thoughts tumbled around inside Rachael's head. But one thing stood out, sharp as a knife. The Whisperer had known this would happen. Somehow, in some impossible way, the old computer at the internet café had made one last terrible prediction.

Dad had said computers were bad for you but he was wrong.

They were deadly.

GABRIEL

'That looks fantastic, Samantha!'

Samantha smiled at her friend Clare. She was
pleased with her collage too. She had worked on it
for days and now that it was finished she was
convinced it was the best thing she'd ever done in
her art lessons.

Several other students came over and admired
her work.

'That's so dark!' whispered one enviously.

Samantha stepped back from her work and inspected it with a critical eye. She had got the pictures of the leering vampires off a great website. They looked truly gruesome! And the gargoyles with their twisted bodies were proper photographs that she'd taken at the local church. The background was a waterfall of blood which she had painted with oils. Samantha was fascinated by anything *dark*. She dressed in black whenever she could, always wore loads of heavy eye make-up and dyed her long, straight hair raven-black. Her friends had been surprised at first, but now everyone seemed to be used to her look.

Samantha knew she had excelled herself with the picture in front of her. Who could possibly not like it?

And that was the trouble. Straight away she could think of someone who wouldn't. Her teacher, Mrs Fluffy-Wuffy-Bunny Butler.

Mrs Butler was so wet she didn't need to shower in the mornings. She was a weak, pale woman who looked as if she had never enjoyed anything in her life. She drifted about her classroom, speaking in a tiny voice and getting anxious when anyone used bold colours. She insisted on having the blinds down on every window because she claimed the sunlight hurt her eyes. What a wuss!

Samantha wished she had her old art teacher this year. Mr Haines would have loved the collage – even though he sometimes joked about her obsession with anything 'Gothic', as he put it.

She was jolted out of her thoughts by a voice behind her.

'Ah, yes, Samantha.' It was Mrs Butler. She squinted through her thick glass lenses at the work in front of her and smiled weakly. 'That looks . . . interesting,' she murmured, and without another glance she wandered on to look at someone else's project.

'Oh, dear,' groaned Clare. 'Did she say "interesting"?'

'We all know what Bunny Butler means by that!'

said Samantha. 'Interesting is her word for rubbish.'

'She just doesn't understand your Goth thing,' said Clare sympathetically.

'I keep telling everyone, we don't call ourselves Goths any more,' laughed Samantha. 'We're Alternatives! But you're right. She doesn't have a clue.'

The lesson was nearly over and Samantha was just putting her collage back into her art case when Mrs Butler tapped faintly on an easel with her pencil. 'Excuse me, everyone,' she announced. 'Erm . . . This week's assignment is entitled "My home". I want you to take your inspiration from something in your house.' She looked over at Samantha. 'I hope you can manage this one, Samantha. Something nice. A vase of pretty flowers perhaps, or a bowl of fruit . . . but no blood oranges!'

Mrs Butler was still tittering at her own feeble joke as the class filed out for lunch.

'See you on the field,' called Clare.

Samantha finished tidying away and slouched

out of the art room. To think she used to look forward to art lessons! It had been her favourite subject until Mrs Butler took over. Still, it was lunch-time now. She shoved her hands in her pockets and her fingers closed round her camera. What better way to cheer herself up than by taking photos of kids at school. But not the usual all-in-a-line, silly-grin-type photos. Samantha preferred to photograph people unawares. That way you got the true image.

'I see you've got your best friend with you as usual!' said a cheerful voice behind her. It was her friend Jessie coming out of the gym. 'Who are you going to creep up on today?'

'Don't be a wally!' Samantha grinned. 'I don't exactly creep up on people. I just wait till they're not looking.'

'Well, I must admit you do get some great shots,' said Jessie. 'But you ought to be careful. One day you'll get so attached to your camera you'll need an operation to separate the two of you!'

But it wasn't a joke to Samantha. She was going to do photography for a living when she left school. But she wasn't going to have a nice cosy little studio and take photos of smoochy wedding couples or grinning babies or girls in frilly ballet outfits. No, she was going to capture people doing real things. Gritty, true-life images.

'You wait,' she told Jessie, 'one day I'll have public exhibitions of my photos and you'll be telling everyone how you went to school with the famous Samantha Tennison.'

'And your pictures will be selling for millions all over the world!' laughed Jessie. 'Anyway, I'm going to see Heather and Clare on the field. Coming?'

'Yeah, catch up with you in a minute,' muttered Samantha, lining up another shot.

She started aiming the camera at people coming out of the building. She got some great shots and then went in search of her friends. She didn't want to spend all lunch-time on her own. But when she came across them she realized she'd found another photo opportunity. Clare was sitting with Heather and Jessie on the field in their usual place. Samantha paused by the corner of the science block and watched them. Heather was scraping Clare's hair right up on top of her head and sticking brightly coloured clips all over it.

She could hear snippets of their conversation.

'Keep your head still, Clare!'

'Ow!'

'You look like a Martian!'

'Dare you to go into class like that!'

Samantha held the camera up and snapped away, taking close-ups of Jessie laughing, Heather with her tongue stuck out in concentration and Clare grimacing in pain as each clip was rammed in.

'Brilliant!' Samantha murmured to herself, as she took photo after photo. 'Three completely different characters and I've caught them just as they are.'

Heather suddenly spotted her and waved. 'Hey, Samantha!' she called. 'Put that camera away. Come here!'

Samantha walked over to join her friends, though she wasn't going to let them come anywhere near her with their glittery clips!

'Come and have your hair done by a top stylist!' ordered Heather. 'Much more fun than taking snaps all day!'

'Not for the client!' laughed Clare, wincing as she pulled clips out.

Samantha grinned and ducked as Heather came at her with a brush. Then she noticed that there was someone leaning against the trunk of the old oak tree that grew at the edge of the field.

Her stomach lurched. It was Gabriel! Gabriel was in her year, and even though they were in the same maths group she had never spoken to him. Not many people had. He was a bit of a loner and some thought he was a weirdo. But that made him all the more attractive to Samantha. He was tall and blond and gorgeous with his dark clothes and mysterious brooding look.

Samantha was surprised that she hadn't spotted

him when she'd been taking the photos of her friends. But he must be in the background of one of them, surely. This was great! She'd actually got him in her camera! If she'd known he was there in front of her, her hand would have been shaking too much to get a clear shot. She couldn't wait to see how many pictures she'd got with him in. She jumped out of Heather's reach and turned the camera back on ready to scroll through. But nothing happened. The screen stayed blank. She must have run out of battery. What bad timing! She didn't have any spares with her. She'd have to wait till she got home and uploaded the photos on to her computer.

When she looked up she realized there was a bunch of Year 8 boys posing in a line in front of her. Their arms were draped round each other's shoulders and they were pulling silly grins.

'Take us! Take us!' they were calling. 'We're supermodels!'

Samantha stuffed her camera back into her pocket.

'Shove off!' she told them cheerily, and they ran away whooping loudly.

'I've had enough of the clips!' said Clare. 'Got your dice with you, Jessie?'

Jessie rummaged in her bag and brought out a huge novelty dice she'd got at a car boot sale. Instead of numbers on each face, there were instructions – *yes, no, argue, go home, kiss* and *dance*. All you had to do was ask the dice a question, throw it and see what the answer was. And you had to do what it said or you would face bad luck all day.

'What have I got for dinner?' asked Heather, throwing the dice.

'*Dance!*' grinned Samantha. 'What a stupid answer!'

'But you've got to do it,' laughed Jessie.

Heather jumped to her feet and did a silly sort of jig. *It would have made a great picture,* thought Samantha. She wished her battery hadn't run out.

Samantha wondered if Gabriel was still leaning by the tree. She tried to sneak a look. He was there and he was staring right back! Their eyes locked. He gazed intently at her for a moment. Then he turned and walked slowly away. What did that mean? she wondered. Could it be that he fancied her as well? Who knew what went on behind that brooding face? She couldn't ask anyone. Gabriel didn't seem to have any mates. Anyway, she didn't want to admit her crush just yet.

'Samantha!' Heather interrupted her thoughts. 'It's your turn to roll the dice. Come on, ask a question and see what the answer is – but you've got to do what it says.'

'I'm not letting some stupid bit of plastic run my life,' grinned Samantha.

'But if you ask the right question it might come true,' said Clare. 'Remember last month when I hadn't done my maths homework and I asked the dice if I would get away with it and it said, *go home*. And I did in the end. I was so worried about what

Mr Lewis would say that I was sick and got sent home before the lesson!'

'What about the time when we were going to the school dance,' piped up Heather with mock seriousness, 'and I didn't know whether to wear my black boots or my brown ones. So I asked the dice and the answer was *kiss*!'

'What was that meant to mean?' asked Samantha, puzzled.

'I don't know,' giggled Heather. 'I wore shoes instead!'

Her friends chatted on, but Samantha had stopped listening. She had more important things to think about. She pictured herself at home sighing over Gabriel's image on her computer screen. She'd crop and enlarge it so that he filled the whole photo. Then she'd print it off and put it under her pillow. Bliss!

Then she realized that Clare was shaking her arm.

'What were you dreaming about?' she asked. 'Or should I say who!'

'Give up, Clare,' laughed Heather. 'Our Samantha will never let you know which boy she fancies.'

'I like to keep you guessing,' said Samantha, smiling at her friends.

If only they knew!

As soon as she got home from school, Samantha slung her bag down in the hall and raced upstairs to the study. She switched the computer on and connected the camera. She couldn't wait to see all her photos – especially Gabriel. But nothing happened.

Then she remembered. 'Batteries!' She scrabbled in a drawer and found the right ones for her camera. The camera whirred into life and the pictures began to upload.

'Come on. Come on!' she muttered at the screen. They seemed to be taking ages. 'When I'm famous I'm going to have a state-of-the-art program that works instantly.'

Luckily she didn't have much homework that

night – just that stupid new art project. She felt cross just thinking about it. 'Something in the home' – how nice and safe. Perhaps she'd paint a picture of a knitted toilet roll cover. Mrs Butler would like that. She probably had them in every room in her house! Then Samantha had a better idea. She would use today's photos of her friends and if Mrs Butler protested she'd say 'home is where your friends are'. She'd seen that on a fridge magnet somewhere. And anyway it would be a safe, 'happy' collage. Then let Bunny Butler try to mark her down for being too dark!

A ping from the computer told her that the photos were ready at last. She scrolled impatiently down to today's shots. Samantha clicked on each in turn, her heart racing. The first few were close-ups so she knew Gabriel wouldn't be in those. Then she got to the wide-angle shots. In the background was the field and the oak tree. But Gabriel wasn't in the first one, or the next. Perhaps he'd come along after those.

'Come on, come on,' she muttered under her breath as she scrolled through. But he wasn't in any of them. What was going on? He must be! She went through them all again, enlarging every section till it blurred. There was no sign of him.

Samantha was annoyed at her bad luck. She'd been sure that Gabriel would appear in at least *one* of the shots. He must have turned up after she'd finished.

Her mum knocked on the door and poked her head into the room. 'Are you busy with your homework?' she asked. 'Or do you want to come and watch TV with me?'

Samantha didn't feel like doing any homework now. Her art collage could wait till tomorrow.

She turned her computer off. 'Coming,' she said.

Samantha felt grumpy all next morning.

'What's the matter?' asked Jessie at lunch-time. 'You're very quiet. Are you feeling all right?'

'Yes.' Samantha managed a grin. It wasn't Jessie's fault after all. 'Just tired,' she said.

But although she was smiling she still felt really bad inside. She probably wouldn't *ever* have another chance to get a photo of Gabriel. And she'd *never* dare speak to him. Supposing she didn't get any further than lusting after him from afar? Life wouldn't be worth living!

It was double maths after lunch. Samantha slouched in and sat down. She cheered up a bit. It wasn't that she enjoyed algebra and trigonometry, but it was the one subject where she and Gabriel were in the same group. Apart from in maths, she was sure of seeing him only at the bus stop. But maths gave her a chance to ogle him for a whole hour. Though you had to be careful in Mr Lewis's class. Their teacher didn't miss much. Samantha had found that if she bent over her work and let her hair flop forwards in a dark curtain she could peer secretly out at Gabriel.

She tried to look casually round so that she could

spy where he was sitting. There he was in the far corner. A bad place for ogling. Mr Lewis walked along to Gabriel's desk. Samantha quickly turned away. She didn't want to be caught staring.

'You don't look too well, Gabriel,' she heard Mr Lewis say. 'You're very pale.'

'I had no lunch,' Gabriel answered simply. His smooth, deep voice sent a thrill through Samantha.

'Why not?' asked his teacher. 'How can you concentrate on your work when you're hungry?'

'The pizzas had garlic in. I'm allergic to garlic.' Samantha could hear one or two students sniggering. But they didn't laugh very loudly. No one would dream of teasing Gabriel about an allergy. Just like Samantha, most people were in awe of him. Samantha opened her exercise book as Mr Lewis walked towards the front of the classroom. She could feel Gabriel's brooding presence behind her. No way was she going to be able to concentrate!

* * *

'What's up with you, then?' Clare linked her arm in Samantha's as they filed out of school with Heather and Jessie at the end of the day. 'You've been on another planet these last few days. Don't tell me you're in love!'

Samantha looked round to make sure there was no one else in earshot. She couldn't hold it in any longer – she had to tell someone!

'It's Gabriel,' she admitted. 'I really fancy him but I don't suppose he even knows I exist. And I don't know what to do.'

Her friends all glanced at each other. Samantha knew Gabriel was the last person *they'd* have a crush on.

'Very convenient,' grinned Jessie, giving Samantha a playful nudge. 'You can worship him from afar, knowing he'll never speak to you.'

'That's not fair,' protested Samantha.

'Then why haven't you got a crush on a normal boy . . .' giggled Heather, '. . . like Daniel?'

Samantha squirmed. Daniel Wilkes had

certainly let her know that he fancied her but she'd done nothing about it. He just didn't have it for her.

'Gabriel is so good-looking and mysterious,' she said. 'Daniel is just boring and . . .'

'Normal?' suggested Clare.

Samantha groaned.

'Normal's good,' said Heather. 'Normal gets you a date. Gabriel might be good-looking but . . .' She shivered. 'He's so cold.'

'Oh, come on,' said Jessie. 'At least Samantha's getting interested in boys at last. I thought she was married to her camera!' Everyone laughed. 'Tell you what,' Jessie went on. 'Why don't you all come round to mine on Friday night? We'll find out what Samantha should do about Gabriel. We'll use my trusty dice.'

'And you've got to promise to do what it says,' grinned Clare, pulling at Samantha's arm.

'Well, I'll agree to come round,' said Samantha, 'but I'm not promising to throw that stupid dice.'

* * *

Samantha walked with her friends as far as her bus stop. She felt a thrill of excitement. Gabriel was in his usual place at the front of the queue. Heather started giggling.

'Go home!' hissed Samantha.

With lots of silly waves and backward glances, her friends set off down the road. Luckily, Gabriel didn't seem to have noticed them. Samantha gazed at his back from her place in the queue. Would she ever dare speak to him?

The bus came and there was the usual scramble to get on. Gabriel went upstairs, but when Samantha went to follow the way was blocked by people coming down. 'No more room,' smiled a girl, so she went and found a seat by an old lady who grumpily moved her shopping for her to sit down. The bus hadn't gone very far when Samantha's mobile rang. She had to struggle to get it out of her bag, her elbows earning her more black looks from the old lady.

'Are you sitting next to him?' screeched a voice. It was Clare.

'No, I'm not,' whispered Samantha crossly. 'He's upstairs.'

She waited while Clare related this to the others. She heard one of them shouting something.

'Heather says, go up and join him,' said Clare.

'No seats!' retorted Samantha and she snapped her phone shut.

But she'd had an idea. She had been so close to getting a picture of Gabriel yesterday that she was determined to try again. She could get a good shot as he got off the bus. She rummaged in her pocket for her camera.

Samantha's phone beeped. It was a text from Jessie. 'r u upstairs now?'

She jabbed at the buttons, 'No', turned her phone off and shoved it in her bag. If her friends kept pestering she'd miss her photo opportunity.

Right, her camera was free and turned on. The battery level looked good, and she took the lens cover off. Although it was a dull day it was light enough not to use a flash. She decided to wait until Gabriel had got on to the pavement or he might hear the whir of the shutter. If she just rested the camera lightly on top of her bag, she could take pictures of anyone in the street and they wouldn't know about it. And her hands wouldn't shake either.

The bus turned into Bancroft Road. This was where Gabriel usually got off. Her heart started beating faster. A whole crowd of people got off here and she anxiously scanned their faces. At last, there was Gabriel, coolly strolling off the bus as if he had all the time in the world. Luckily the traffic was bad so the bus couldn't pull out straight away. Now Gabriel was on the pavement waiting for a man who was holding a toddler and struggling to open a pushchair. Perfect! This was Samantha's chance. But Gabriel's face was half hidden by the upturned collar of his long black overcoat. If only he would turn in her direction! There was no point taking a picture if she couldn't see his face.

'Get a move on!' came a voice. A fierce-looking man with a pit bull terrier on a lead had come up behind Gabriel and was pushing past him. Samantha was astonished to see that the man's dog suddenly cowered away from Gabriel. Its spiked collar pulled the skin on its neck into folds and it was whimpering. It looked terrified. What on earth was wrong with it?

'Come here, you stupid dog!' yelled the owner, trying to drag the cringing terrier along. The other man had dropped the pushchair and was now holding his wailing child up high out of the way. Other people were shouting.

'Get that dog out of here!'

'What's the matter with him?'

'Should be muzzled!'

In the midst of all this stood Gabriel. Far from panicking like everyone else, he had a slight smile round his lips as he stared calmly at the dog. He was so cool. Ultra cool! This amazing scene would make a good photo but Samantha was only interested in Gabriel. She forgot all about her plans to balance the camera on her bag. She pulled it up to her face and peered through the viewfinder. Now she had a great shot of his face! She snapped away, leaning across her neighbour.

'Do you mind? I've got eggs in that bag!'

The old woman had a face like thunder. Samantha muttered an apology and sat back. But she felt wonderful. She had her photos of Gabriel! The bus began to pull away and she couldn't resist taking one last look at him.

She jumped in surprise. He was staring straight at her, just like he had on the school field! She turned away in confusion. His stare made her shiver. It was as if he knew what she'd been doing. But he hadn't noticed, had he? She hadn't used a flash, after all. She quickly put her camera away. She'd look at the photos when she got home. It would be the first thing she did.

She jumped off the bus as soon as it got to her

stop and ran up her road to her house. But as she opened the front door her mother grabbed her.

'You've got to help,' she told her. 'I was held up at work and I'll never get to my yoga class at this rate. Can you empty the dishwasher and keep an eye on the spaghetti bolognese? I'm going to hang up the washing.' And she disappeared before Samantha could protest.

At last the kitchen was clear, she'd had dinner and her mother had gone. Samantha had just started to climb the stairs up to the study when the doorbell rang. She could hear giggling from outside. She knew who that was.

'Hi!' beamed Clare, as she burst in, followed by Heather and Jessie. They'd ridden over on their bikes. 'Can you come out? We're going to get a burger.'

'We can show you the questions you've got to ask the dice on Friday,' added Jessie.

All Samantha wanted to do was go upstairs and

look at her photographs. 'I can't,' she sighed. 'I've already eaten and . . . I've too much to do.'

'Well, have a look at the questions now,' insisted Jessie, rummaging in her pockets and pulling out a tatty piece of paper.

Samantha took the paper.

'"Should Samantha tell Gabriel he's gorgeous?"' she read out loud. 'As if! "Will Gabriel be a great kisser?" Well, I won't be telling you lot if he is!' She pretended to peer closely at the list. 'This one looks more interesting.'

'Which one's that?' asked Heather eagerly. 'I bet it's mine.'

'It says, "Should my friends leave me alone and get themselves to the burger bar?"'

Jessie snatched the paper back. 'All right, but you're not getting away with it on Friday,' she grinned. 'That dice will be waiting for you!'

The three of them went off, giggling.

At last Samantha had the house to herself. She ran up the stairs to the study and turned the PC on.

By now she was desperate to get her pictures uploaded and see how Gabriel had turned out. Then she would print off a copy of the best photo.

The pictures slowly appeared on the screen. Samantha scrolled down to the ones she'd taken at the bus stop. There was the father with the pushchair, the cowering dog and the fierce-looking man. And there was another and another, but no sign of Gabriel in any of them. And yet he'd been right in the middle of the scene. She couldn't understand it: this time she knew he had been in the viewfinder. She'd been aiming her camera at him and him alone. But all she could see in these pictures was a shadowy, blurred outline of . . . something. He couldn't have been moving every time she clicked the shutter, surely. In fact, she was certain he hadn't. He had just stood there being cool.

She sat back in her chair and stared at the screen. She knew that Gabriel should have been in every picture. A cold feeling began to creep up her spine.

A horrible idea came into her head and she could not get rid of it. Gabriel didn't appear in photos. He didn't like garlic. And now she came to think about it, she had never seen him standing in sunlight. Could Gabriel be a vampire?

'Don't be so ridiculous,' Samantha told herself. She was being stupid. OK, there were loads of websites about vampires, but they were just made by nutters. Weren't they? And anyway, vampires never came out in the day. Gabriel *did*.

Then suddenly the image of the fierce dog cowering and cringing came into her mind. Was it Gabriel that had scared it? She knew from the internet that animals were scared by ghosts. Were they also scared by vampires?

Samantha knew if her mum or any of her friends knew what she was thinking they'd tell her not to be silly. But she'd spent so much time thinking about Gabriel recently that she couldn't persuade herself to shake off this feeling. There was only one way to set her mind at rest. She'd just have to prove to herself that Gabriel wasn't a vampire. After all, she didn't want to have a crush on a bloodsucking monster! It wouldn't hurt to check him out. But she had to be sure of her facts.

She went on the internet and found a website that looked as if it might help. It was called Fearsome Fang Facts and it was dark with lots of blood dripping down the screen. Perfect. Samantha clicked on the messageboard but then she hesitated. She felt a bit stupid asking what the best way was to test whether someone is a vampire.

She scrolled down the recent entries. Brilliant! There it was. Someone had already asked a similar thing.

'there is an old man down our street wot is mean and pale and never comes out in daylight how can i find out if hes a vampire'

And someone else had answered.

'Vampires have no reflection. Hope that helps. Keep us posted if you're still alive, ha ha!'

So all she had to do was find out if Gabriel had a reflection in a mirror. There, it was all sorted.

By Friday morning, Samantha had tried to talk herself out of the vampire idea. But it wouldn't go away. She hadn't had any opportunity to do the test. They hadn't had any classes together and she couldn't do it at the bus stop! But the first lesson today was maths and this time Gabriel was sitting in front of her. She could spend the whole lesson gazing at him! It was just a pity that this corner of the classroom was so gloomy. In fact, did Gabriel always sit as far away from the sunlight as possible? She thought he probably did. She mentally shook herself. She had to stop this vampire nonsense. Everyone always said she had a dark and overactive imagination.

But a little part of her still wanted to try the reflection test. In an instant she could prove to herself once and for all that Gabriel was a normal boy. What harm could it do?

She took out her little make-up mirror and pretended to be removing a rogue eyelash. Then gradually she swivelled the mirror around. It was hard to get the angle so that she could see Gabriel's reflection without people realizing what she was up to. How embarrassing would that be! Her mirror was curved, so nothing was very clear if you weren't close to it. At first she got a blurry image of the wall and then of her other hand resting on the desk. She was finding it hard to keep the mirror steady in her excitement. Nearly there.

At this moment the sun came out from behind a cloud. Gabriel leaped to his feet with a cry. Samantha dropped the mirror.

'What's going on over there?' asked Mr Lewis, alarmed.

'Something stung me!' Gabriel said, his hand gripping the back of his neck.

Several of the girls squealed and looked around in case there was a wasp.

'Do you need anything?' asked Mr Lewis. 'Do you want to go to the school nurse?'

'No,' Gabriel answered curtly. 'It doesn't hurt much.' He sat down.

Samantha picked up her mirror and shoved it back in her bag. The sun must have reflected off it and the pinpoint of light had burned Gabriel. She grabbed her pen and tried to concentrate on her geometry.

At lunch-time, Samantha sat in the canteen with her friends. She was worried. The idea that Gabriel was a vampire wouldn't go away. She still hadn't proved he had a reflection. And had she burned him or had it just been the sunlight touching his skin that had made him jump? She could be in danger. Everybody could be in danger. The thought made her shiver.

'Sleepover tonight,' Jessie reminded them all. 'And it's going to be a good one!'

'What time do you want us?' asked Clare.

'How about six?' said Jessie. 'Is that OK, everyone?'

'Great,' said Heather. 'I'll come straight after my dance class.'

'What about you, Samantha?' asked Jessie.

Samantha was only half listening.

'She's still mooning over Gorgeous Gabriel!' whispered Clare.

'This is getting serious!' exclaimed Heather. She waved her hands in front of Samantha's eyes. 'Hello. Earth to Samantha. Is anybody there?'

Samantha grinned sheepishly at them all.

'You've just won an award,' said Heather solemnly.

'What for?'

Heather winked at the others. 'Biggest crush in school!'

Samantha sighed. 'I'm sorry,' she said. 'I can't help it. It's just that . . .'

'It's just that you're desperate about Gabriel and you don't dare do anything about it,' said Clare, putting her arm round her friend.

'Not exactly,' Samantha tried to explain. 'But I'm worried that he . . .'

'. . . will never find out that you fancy him?' finished Jessie.

'And that's where we come in,' added Heather before Samantha could protest. 'There's only one way to solve this. One of us will go and tell him how you feel. How about that?'

'NO!' Samantha slammed her hands down on the table so hard that the cutlery shook. 'That's the last thing anyone must do!'

Her friends stared at her, shocked.

'OK, OK,' said Clare soothingly. 'What's the big deal?'

'You're not worried we might steal him, are you?' asked Heather. 'Don't worry – none of us would want to get in first. Gabriel's yours as far as we're concerned.' She shuddered. 'I've told you, he spooks me out.'

'Of course I know you wouldn't steal him,' Samantha said in a low voice. 'You're my best mates.' She took a deep breath. She had to tell her friends the truth. She was going to have to admit what was really bothering her, however ridiculous it sounded. 'The problem is . . . I think Gabriel's a vampire.'

There. She'd said it. As soon as the words were out of her mouth she wished she'd never spoken. Her friends were looking at her as if she was crazy. And maybe she was. She had to tell them the reasons. Then perhaps they'd understand.

'He doesn't like garlic,' she gabbled, feeling really stupid. 'He always sits in the darkest corner of the classroom. And then there was this pit bull who was terrified of him. He doesn't appear in photos and I bet he doesn't have a reflection! I've tried to find out but it didn't work.'

She went on to tell them how she had burned Gabriel's neck in maths.

'You're just being daft!' said Heather, when she'd finished. 'I know I said he spooks me out but that's ridiculous!'

'And there's loads of people who don't like garlic,' added Jessie. '*I* can't stand it, and I'm not a vampire. At least, I don't think so.' She lunged forward and pretended to bite Samantha on the neck. Heather and Clare giggled, but Samantha jumped angrily out of the way.

'Sorry!' Jessie looked taken aback. 'Only a joke.'

'You mustn't worry about it, Samantha,' Clare tried to reassure her. 'He could easily have been out of the frame when you took the photos – and I bet it wasn't the light that upset him in maths. It probably was a wasp like he said.'

'Come on!' said Heather. 'If we're talking about people who won't go out in the sunlight, then it's Mrs Butler who's the vampire, not Gabriel!'

'Imagine that wispy little soul with fangs,' guffawed Jessie. 'She's more likely to faint at the sight of blood than drink it!'

The three friends fell about laughing.

'You've got to take this seriously,' pleaded

Samantha. 'It sounds really weird but what if I'm right?'

'I know what you're doing!' said Heather suddenly. 'You're just winding us up with this vampire story so you can carry on lusting after Gabriel but not ever try to get a date with him!'

'It makes him even more unavailable,' agreed Jessie. 'Even a Goth like you – sorry, *Alternative* – wouldn't really want to go out with a vampire!'

'I've got the answer!' exclaimed Clare, waving her hands about excitedly. 'We'll ask the dice tonight. Is Gabriel vampire or love interest? That should settle it.'

'Supposing he's good at lovebites,' said Heather. 'He could be both!'

Clare and Jessie shrieked with laughter and even Samantha couldn't help smiling. Now she was glad she'd told her friends about her fears. They were right. All the things that had happened had a perfectly logical explanation. There were no such things as vampires.

Samantha suddenly had the feeling someone was staring at her. She looked up. It was Gabriel! He was sitting on the other side of the canteen. Samantha looked quickly away. But had she imagined it? Had he been smiling at her?

That night, the four of them sat on Jessie's bed. Empty trays of Chinese takeaway were scattered all over the floor and Heather had just produced a big box of chocolates.

Jessie held the dice. 'Should Samantha get Gabriel's phone number?' she said in a solemn voice and then threw the dice into the air. There was no doubt about the answer – *yes*. Samantha's friends laughed.

'My turn,' said Clare, grabbing the dice. 'And what should she do after that?'

'*KISS*'! Heather had a giggling fit and nearly fell off the bed.

Jessie put the dice into Samantha's hands. 'It's going well,' she said. 'You do it now.'

Samantha shrugged. She might as well go with the flow. She knew the others wouldn't shut up until she did. And it was only a bit of fun.

'Does Gabriel know I like him?' she asked with a grin. She flung the dice high into the air. It turned over and over, bounced off the bed, landed on the floor and finally came to rest at the open door.

There was someone standing in the doorway. Someone very tall, wearing black trainers, black jeans and a long black coat.

It was Gabriel! He bent down and carefully picked up the dice between his thumb and forefinger. '*Yes*,' he read. He looked at each of the girls in turn. 'But what was the question?'

Samantha knew her face was bright red. Had Gabriel heard or not? What was he doing here? Had Jessie and co. set her up?

Then she caught sight of Jessie's mum hovering on the landing.

'Erm, Jessie,' she called, sounding a bit

125

concerned. 'This boy says he's a friend of yours . . . and that he was coming straight up.' She sounded unsure.

Samantha looked at Jessie. Her friend appeared as surprised as she was at Gabriel's sudden arrival. She hoped Jessie wouldn't turn him away. But Jessie grinned.

'It's OK, Mum,' she called. 'It's Gabriel – from our school.'

Samantha felt a shiver. Excitement – or was it nerves?

Gabriel strode across the room and sat on the chair in the corner. He nodded at them all. This was the most friendly Samantha had ever seen him. It was great . . . but she had no idea what to do next. She could feel her friends' eyes on her – and it didn't help!

'I've seen you lot around,' said Gabriel, leaning back casually. 'And as we're almost neighbours I thought I should get to know you all.' He gazed at Samantha as if to say 'especially you'. It made

Samantha tingle. She felt as if she could hardly breathe. She wished she could gaze at him and listen to his voice for ever. He looked even more gorgeous than usual – and she'd never been this close before. She was glad she'd worn her new black strappy top and put a dark-red streak in her hair. He'd only seen her in school uniform up till now.

Samantha's stomach was turning cartwheels. This was her chance to speak to Gabriel and she didn't know what to say!

Neither did anybody else, it seemed. There was an awkward silence. Gabriel was the only one who didn't appear bothered by it. He just sat there, turning the dice over and over in his hands.

'Er . . . right . . .' said Jessie uncertainly. 'We're just hanging out . . . erm . . .' She shoved the box of chocolates at him. 'D'you want one?'

'Not now.'

Silence again. *I must do something*, thought Samantha. *But what?*

Jessie suddenly stood up. 'I'll get everyone a drink!' she said brightly. 'Coffee OK?' She made for the door.

'I'll help!' squeaked Heather, bouncing off the bed.

'And me.' Clare was out of the room behind them in an instant.

Samantha knew what was going on. Her friends were leaving her alone with Gabriel on purpose. She felt terrified and excited at the same time.

They sat not speaking for a while. It must be so obvious that her friends had deliberately left them on their own together. But she didn't know what to say to break the silence. Then Gabriel got to his feet. *Oh, no*, thought Samantha, *he's leaving*. But instead of making for the door, he came to sit next to her on the bed!

'I've seen you around a lot recently,' he said, as he leaned back on one elbow.

'Have you?' croaked Samantha. This was ridiculous. She had to pull herself together. But he had noticed her! She went wobbly at the thought.

'You look a bit different from everyone else. More . . . interesting. And you always have a camera with you, taking photos of people when they're not looking.' He paused. 'Have you been taking pictures of me?'

Samantha felt her face go red again. She wanted to deny it. But somehow she couldn't bring herself to lie to Gabriel.

'I . . . well . . . yes, I've tried,' she stammered. 'You're a good subject. I . . . I like you.'

'I thought so,' said Gabriel slowly. 'I don't usually let people take my picture. I'm surprised you didn't know that.' He shook his head at her as if he was angry but then he gave a small smile. 'I hate seeing myself in photos,' he admitted, 'but doesn't everyone?'

'You don't have to worry.' Samantha blurted it out before she could think. 'I didn't get any pictures of you at all. I tried but you never seemed to show up when I checked the images.' She was annoyed to hear a tremor in her voice and Gabriel obviously heard it as well. He gazed at her intently. Samantha felt as if she could drown in those deep-blue eyes.

'Why do you think that is?' he asked at last. Samantha looked at the floor in confusion. She was determined not to admit her silly theory about him. But his next words caught her by surprise.

'What's the matter?' he said, suddenly bringing his face close to hers. 'Do you think I'm some kind of vampire?'

Samantha gasped. He must have read her mind! Was he upset? She made herself look up at him. He was smiling broadly at her. Samantha had never seen him smile in such a friendly manner before. He looked even more gorgeous and now she could see that there wasn't a sign of a fang anywhere in his mouth.

'Of course I don't,' she said. 'Well, not really. But it has been a bit strange . . .' She gulped. 'You don't seem to like the sunlight and you say you're allergic to garlic, and that pit bull the other day was terrified of you.'

To her amazement, Gabriel roared with laughter. Samantha relaxed.

'Yes, I know,' she grinned. 'I let my imagination run riot. I've been reading too much on the internet. Of course there are no such things as vampires . . .'

Gabriel stopped laughing so suddenly it took her aback. 'You don't know how wrong you are,' he told her seriously. 'I may not be one, but I assure you vampires do exist.'

Samantha gaped at him. 'How do you know that?' she asked. 'Have you ever seen one?' She forgot all about being shy in her eagerness to find out more.

'Of course I have,' nodded Gabriel. 'I'm fascinated by them.'

This was great! She wasn't going to find it hard to talk to him now. Not only were they both interested in vampires but it sounded like he was an expert!

'You'll have seen them too,' he went on. 'One of them teaches at our school.'

'You're kidding me!' Samantha exclaimed. Then she thought about it. 'It's Mr Sharp, isn't it! That would explain the dreadful beard. He's probably hiding his fangs under it. No, wait, there's that terrible dinner lady, the one with the tattoos . . .'

But Gabriel shook his head. 'You're way off the mark. Think about it. Who always has the blinds down in her room?'

'You don't mean Bunny Butler!' Samantha almost shrieked. 'You're not telling me she's a vampire! She's feeble and fluffy and . . . so heavily into pink. You're having me on!'

'I wish I was,' answered Gabriel. 'But it's true. The pink is just a decoy. After all, she'd never attract any victims if she swooshed around with a black cloak and asked if she could have a nibble of people's necks. Vampires have to live undercover or they'd be hunted down and have a stake put through their heart.'

'Or a silver bullet,' added Samantha. 'Though I've often wondered where you'd get a silver bullet from.'

'Exactly,' agreed Gabriel. 'A stake is always a better option!'

'But wait a minute,' said Samantha. She suddenly wondered if Gabriel was just taking the mickey. 'How come Bunny Butler survives in daytime? In the films vampires turn to dust in the light.'

But Gabriel didn't seem to be laughing at her. He was engrossed in his subject.

'That's just Hollywood,' he said seriously. 'But vampires are certainly weakened by the sunlight. If they want to go around during the day they have to do overtime with the bloodsucking at night.'

'If that's true, why would Mrs Butler bother with teaching?' asked Samantha, frowning. 'Sounds too risky. If it was me I'd just stay in my coffin all day and wait for nightfall.'

'Mrs Butler uses the daytime to size up her victims and, as they all know her, they won't be scared if they meet her after dark – until it's too late.'

Samantha shuddered. She remembered how her art teacher had crept up behind her to look at her work on more than one occasion. She was probably seeing how juicy the veins in her neck were!

'So are we all in danger, then?' she said.

'Some are,' Gabriel answered. 'But not you. I'll make sure of that.'

Samantha felt a thrill of excitement and she couldn't stop a huge smile spreading over her face. He wanted to protect her! He wouldn't say that unless he really liked her.

They heard footsteps on the stairs and then giggling. It must be her friends with the coffee. Samantha nodded at the door. 'That lot think I'm mad with all my ideas about vampires,' she told Gabriel. 'If you tell them about Bunny Butler, they'll have to believe it.'

'No!' exclaimed Gabriel, jumping up. 'I've a better idea. Let's keep it to ourselves for the moment.'

He held out a hand. She took it. It felt warm and strong. 'Would you like to go for a walk?'

Samantha nodded eagerly. Gabriel flung the bedroom door open. Clare fell into the room and Jessie nearly threw her tray of mugs in the air.

'Drinks anyone?' grinned Heather.

'No, thanks,' said Gabriel. He took Samantha by the hand and led her past her gawping friends and down towards the front door. 'We're going out.'

As Samantha got to the door she glanced back. Jessie, Heather and Clare were all standing at the top of the stairs. They looked pleased. Clare gave her the thumbs-up. *They're really good mates*, thought Samantha. She knew she'd never have got this far without their help. They'd done her such a favour. She waved happily at them and walked out into the night with Gabriel.

'So where are we going?' asked Samantha as they strolled down the road. She couldn't believe it. She was actually holding hands with a boy – and a gorgeous one at that. It was a lovely night. The moon was full. Just right for a romantic walk. This was much better than playing a silly dice game.

'Let's go towards the church,' suggested Gabriel as they got to the end of Jessie's road and turned the corner. 'If you're very lucky I'll show you where Mrs Butler lives.'

That would really be something to tell her friends about, thought Samantha. With any luck they might even spot her coffin, if the frilly curtains weren't closed. But supposing Bunny Butler saw them!

'Won't that be dangerous?' she asked. They were passing the church graveyard now. The streetlights made strange shadows among the graves. She knew Gabriel had promised to protect her, but even so she was beginning to feel uneasy.

'I told you, you're safe with me,' Gabriel reassured her. 'I won't let Mrs Butler jump on you.'

Samantha felt comforted for a moment. But she couldn't stop herself glancing into the churchyard as they passed it. She would certainly never have gone anywhere near it at night if she'd been on her own.

'Do you think there are vampires in there?' Samantha whispered, pointing. This eerie place seemed a perfect haunt for them.

'We'll check it out.' Gabriel opened the church gate and led her through.

Samantha stepped reluctantly on to the graveyard path. 'I don't know if I want to. Can't we just stick to the road?'

It was one thing reading about vampires on the internet but quite another actually coming face to face with one.

'Where's your sense of adventure?' scoffed Gabriel, shutting the gate behind her. 'Anyway, this is a short cut. We can take the path through Norsely Wood to Mrs Butler's house.'

Samantha felt she had little choice. If she wanted to go out with this gorgeous guy it was clear she was going to have to take some risks. She held tightly to Gabriel's hand as they made their way among the graves. She looked right and left, and then behind her. She felt a shiver of fear. How exactly could Gabriel protect her if a vampire did come? Did he have a wooden stake or a secret store of garlic with him? As they got further away from the road, it grew darker and darker. The moon had disappeared behind a cloud and they were far from the streetlights now.

Suddenly something jerked through the air and swooped past Samantha's cheek as it flew off into the night. She screamed and clung to Gabriel.

'It's only a bat,' he laughed. He put his arm round her. 'Don't worry, Samantha. You won't be scared for much longer. We're nearly in the woods.'

Samantha felt safer with his arm around her. It was nice. She was almost glad she'd been scared by the bat. She wished she knew more about being on a date. Was Gabriel going to kiss her? She hoped so . . . but not in the graveyard.

She was relieved when they came to the archway

in the churchyard wall and made their way into the woods beyond. The moon had come out again and the trees were pale in its light. It was much more romantic than being among the graves. They walked along the footpath. Samantha had been in Norsely Wood many times when she was little. She'd ridden her bike here, jumped the stream that ran along the side of the path and picked blackberries with her mum. But she'd never been here after dark. She'd had no idea her art teacher lived anywhere near the wood. She began to wonder how many more vampires there were at school. Or even living down her own road!

'So who else is a vampire?' she asked Gabriel, as they walked together along the narrow path.

'Well, there's Brian Waldham,' he told her. 'And probably all the others in the football team by now. Then there's Cass Elliot and Neil Sheridan and . . .'

'I sat right next to Neil in geography yesterday!' Samantha shuddered at the thought. 'I suppose he *has* been looking pale lately. He said he's just getting over glandular fever.'

'He's not likely to tell you he's a bloodsucking monster, is he?' grinned Gabriel, squeezing her shoulder. 'Sniffy McCann's another one. And Mary Logan.'

Samantha shook her head in amazement. 'I'd never have guessed. But how do you know all this?'

'I can't tell you that,' said Gabriel. 'You don't want to know. I just recognize them, that's all. You have to trust me.' He stopped and turned to face her. 'You do trust me, don't you?'

Samantha looked up into his eyes and felt spellbound by his gaze.

'Yes,' she whispered. 'Of course I trust you.'

'Don't worry about vampires,' he murmured as he bent his head towards her. 'I won't let any of them near you.'

Here we go, thought Samantha. She realized Gabriel had never had any intention of taking her to see Mrs Butler's house. That was just a trick to get her into the woods for a kiss! Which was all right by her. Samantha hoped she'd know what to do when their lips met. She raised her face to his.

Suddenly there was a horrible hissing noise. It sounded very close.

'What's that?' Samantha squealed and, without thinking, leaped back out of his embrace. An unearthly wailing filled the air.

But Gabriel just turned slowly and glanced down the path. 'Well, it's certainly not a vampire,' he said.

Samantha peered round him. There on the dark path, hissing and spitting as if its life depended on it, was a small, terrified cat. Its hackles were raised and it began to back away.

'We can't have a kitty interrupting us, can we?' Gabriel said, frowning.

He took a step towards it. The cat turned and sped off, howling at the top of its voice. Gabriel chased after it and disappeared from sight.

Now it was strangely quiet in the woods. The trees seemed to lean in at her in an eerie way.

Samantha wondered how she could have found the woods romantic. They were desolate. She felt as if she was the last thing alive. And where was Gabriel? Surely he didn't need to have chased the cat right away. She peered through the dark but she couldn't see anything.

'Gabriel?' she whispered. He had gone and left her, after all his talk of protection, and it wasn't funny. There could be vampires right here, hiding behind the trees. Or even more bats! Samantha was all alone. And scared.

There was the noise of a twig breaking behind her. It sounded like a gunshot. Samantha jumped and whirled round just as a tall shape loomed up out of the dark.

'Did you miss me?'

It was Gabriel.

'But how come you're behind me . . .' spluttered Samantha. 'You went that way!' She pointed over her shoulder.

'I must have taken a wrong turn chasing that

stupid moggy away,' smiled Gabriel. 'Now where were we?'

He stepped forward and put both his hands on her shoulders. Samantha tried to smile up at him but Gabriel seemed different.

'I . . . er,' she tried to speak. 'I'm not in the mood . . . I got scared . . . you left me . . . there could have been vampires.'

The pressure of his hands on her shoulders became harder, painful. Samantha tried to pull away but his grip just tightened.

'Vampires are the least of your worries,' he said. Samantha suddenly went cold. Gabriel's voice had changed. It was deeper and rasping. 'It is not good to offend me.'

He straightened up and she shrank away from him. He was taller than before. In fact, he was growing in front of her eyes! How could this be? He was now taller than any man she had ever seen. She struggled in terror but she couldn't get free of his grasp.

'What?' he sneered. 'Leaving so soon?' Samantha didn't recognize his voice at all now. It was impossibly deep and seemed to fill the woods. She couldn't tear her gaze away from his face. There was a glowing red light in his eyes, burning into hers, keeping her hypnotized.

'You should have been more careful who you took pictures of,' he snarled. 'You should ask permission. You never know who your subject may turn out to be.'

'I'm sorry!' whimpered Samantha. 'I'll never do it again. Please, please, let me go now.' But Gabriel's grip just tightened. How could she ever get away from this nightmare?

She slumped down as if she was fainting. It caught Gabriel by surprise and he loosened his grip for a second. But that second was enough. Samantha pulled free and ran as fast as she could. She would rather face bats and vampires than the thing that Gabriel had become. She sped along the path, stumbling in the dark. Her breath was coming out in sobs. But she was free! She would run to Jessie's. Her friends would still be there, sitting on the bed, playing with that silly dice. If only she'd stayed with them! But she was a fast runner. And she had a head start. She could get to Jessie's house, and safety.

Then somehow Gabriel was standing in front of Samantha, blocking her path. How had he done that? Surely it wasn't possible.

'Get away from me!' she screamed. She tried to dart round him, but in an instant he had seized her arms. He was so tall now that he blotted everything out. She tried to struggle but he held her so firmly she couldn't move. His whole body shone with a green glow and in this strange light she could see his forehead bulging and swelling. With a noise that sounded like the cracking of bone, two thick horns burst out of his head. His skin had grown hard and scaly. She looked down at his hands grasping her in an iron grip and saw the yellow nails begin to lengthen and curl like claws round her wrists. A horrible smell filled her nostrils and she thought she was going to be sick. The Gabriel she had fancied from afar had completely disappeared. Now he was a monster.

Gabriel gave a sneering laugh.

'What a silly girl!' his booming voice mocked her. 'Trying to run away!'

'What are you?' whispered Samantha in terror. 'Are you a vampire?'

Gabriel threw back his head and roared. 'Vampires quake at my approach,' he snarled. 'Vampires cower before me. I am much more than a vampire. I have been on earth since man first walked. None is more powerful than I. Some call me . . . a demon.'

Samantha barely heard him. She couldn't take her eyes from his.

Slowly the demon's mouth opened.

Samantha felt a terrible weakness flood over her. Her arms and legs seemed to turn to lead and her head was swimming. With a last desperate effort, she tore her gaze from his eyes and looked down at her body. A thin plume of vapour was emanating from her. It was drifting up towards Gabriel's gaping mouth.

My energy, she thought. *He's taking my very essence!*

As her soul was sucked from her body, Gabriel's form became transparent for an instant. Samantha was aware of distorted impressions of people writhing inside him. Each face was twisted in terrible pain and each victim was howling in torment.

Samantha felt her eyes close and the last breath shudder from her body. Gabriel had taken her soul, as he had taken millions of souls before hers.

FAST
FORWARD

The queue for the Timewarp nightclub stretched
right down the road and round the corner. Jake
looked up at the flashing neon sign over the door.
'Sixteen To Eighteens Night', it said.

'Do you think we'll get in?' he asked Oliver.

'Sure to this time,' grinned Oliver. 'After all, we're
nearly sixteen.'

'Well, we're three weeks nearer than last time we
came here!' said Jake grimly. He checked out the

bouncers. He didn't fancy getting into a tussle with them!

Timewarp was THE place to go on Friday nights. The queue was full of familiar faces from Jake's year at school – and most of them were only fifteen like him and Oliver. But unlike Jake and his friend they all looked much older. Especially the girls. All *they* had to do was slap on a bit of make-up and everyone thought they were at least seventeen. And even boys they knew were younger than them got in! Still, Jake and Oliver hoped they had a chance this week. They were both wearing their trendiest T-shirts and jeans and Jake had gelled his hair. But Oliver was short and baby-faced, and although Jake was tall he was thin and knew he looked a bit weedy.

Jake spotted Courtney Wilson further down the queue. She was sure to be with her mates. And that meant Fran would be there. Courtney Wilson was hard and loud and so were most of her friends. But Fran was different. She was blonde and pretty and she wasn't such a loud mouth as Courtney. Well, he'd never actually spoken to her but she looked nice. He wondered if he would have the nerve to ask her out. He'd never dare at school but maybe in the darkness of the nightclub . . .? There she was – and she was looking his way! For a moment their eyes met. Jake thought his heart was going to stop! He tried to grin at her, but someone made a joke and she turned away, laughing.

It was awful waiting, not knowing if they were going to get in. Jake began to fidget nervously. Some boys up ahead were being turned away. *I'm sure I look older than them*, thought Jake.

Rebecca from his class was in front of them. She had a red cap on. Oliver gave Jake a nudge. He reached forward and whipped it off her head. Then he put it on and did a silly dance to amuse everybody. Rebecca rolled her eyes but Jake couldn't help laughing. Oliver was now strutting up and down the queue doing a robotic walk.

'What babies!'

Jake stopped laughing. Courtney Wilson and all her mates had gathered round to watch. And they didn't look impressed.

'They *so* don't look sixteen.'

'Like either of them have a chance of being let in.'

'They need to grow up!'

'Stop it!' laughed Fran. 'They're only having a bit of fun.'

Jake slipped back into the queue, trying to look invisible. Rebecca glared at them both and snatched her cap back.

But Courtney hadn't finished.

'Ah, look at the little toddlers, girls,' she mocked. 'Want to go in the big boys' club?' She grinned back at her sniggering friends. 'Little Jakie and Ollie here should get themselves down the fair instead. They can go on the baby rides with Mickey Mouse and Dumbo!'

Now everyone was laughing. Jake wanted to run away. But then the queue started to move. He couldn't give up now. They were nearly at the door.

'Think cool,' he muttered to himself. 'We'll show Courtney and her friends! They won't be laughing when we go straight inside.'

A burly doorman in a leather jacket stood on the step. His mate stood behind him. He waved through the group ahead and now it was Jake and Oliver's turn. Jake put his hands in his pockets and began to whistle casually. Oliver straightened his shoulders and tried to make himself look tall.

The doorman looked them up and down, shook his head and jerked a thumb towards the road. Jake pretended not to notice and went to go up the steps, but his way was barred by a large hand.

'You're not old enough,' growled the doorman. 'Neither of you. Hop it!'

Jake knew there was no point arguing. He could hear the sniggering from Courtney and her gang. But they stopped as soon as they got to the bouncers. They strolled casually up the steps and swept straight into the club, smiling at the doormen as they went. Jake watched bitterly as Fran followed the others inside.

'Have a nice evening, girls,' the doorman called after them.

Jake and Oliver plodded off down the road. Some boys from the year above went by, full of the fantastic night they were about to have in Timewarp.

'School's going to be really great on Monday!' groaned Jake. 'They'll never let us forget this.'

'Don't worry about them!' said Oliver. 'What shall we do instead? Fancy some chips?' That was Oliver all over. He never worried about anything. He was always cheerful.

And he usually managed to cheer Jake up – but not tonight. Jake felt anger simmering inside him. He ducked down an alleyway at the side of the club and beckoned to Oliver. 'Let's go round the back and try to get in through a window.'

Oliver stood on the corner. 'What's the point?' he

shrugged. 'They'll just chuck us out again when they find us. Good entertainment for the clubbers – not so good for us!'

Jake knew Oliver was right. He mooched back to join his friend and the two of them set off again along the street.

'If only I was shaving,' Jake muttered. 'Then I'd look sixteen. And Courtney and her friends wouldn't have so much to laugh about!' Jake checked his chin every morning in the mirror but so far he had not found a single hair. He tried shaving anyway, but it just left him with a rash.

'I wouldn't take any notice of their teasing,' said Oliver brightly. 'You should enjoy being young. It doesn't last long. You're grown up for a lot longer!'

'That's a great help!' grumbled Jake. 'Perhaps you'd like to tell Courtney.'

Suddenly they heard a shout behind them. 'Jake! Oliver! Wait a minute!'

They turned to see a small figure running down the road towards them. It was Megan.

Megan was in the same class as them. But if they looked young for their age, Megan had twice the problem. She was tiny! Some people thought she was only twelve – and she acted even younger.

'Let's wait,' said Oliver, waving at her. 'She can hang out with us.'

'Oh, no,' groaned Jake. 'She'll make us look like a nursery school outing.'

'Don't be daft,' said Oliver as Megan caught up with them. 'The three of us can have a laugh together.'

'I saw you get turned away from the club,' panted Megan. 'I was on my way to the fair.'

'Let's all do something together,' suggested Oliver. 'Courtney suggested we toddle off to the fair. We could go with you.'

'Great idea!' exclaimed Megan, grinning like a two-year-old.

Jake thought about it. It had to be better than going home at eight o'clock on a Friday night – and they'd probably have a laugh anyway. Just as long as Courtney and her gang didn't find out and make endless Dumbo and Mickey Mouse jokes.

'OK,' he agreed. 'What are we waiting for?'

The fair was huge and noisy. There were flashing lights of all colours and laser beams swinging around the dark sky. They could hear a blur of distorted music and people screaming excitedly from every ride. The air was full of the smell of burgers, fried onions and candy floss.

'This will be fun!' shouted Oliver, as they pushed their way through the crowds between the carousel and the rifle range. 'Better than that silly nightclub.'

Jake looked up at the Big Wheel, turning slowly above their heads. It seemed to be full of boys with their girlfriends. *How romantic*, he thought. Well, if he didn't have a chance with Fran, maybe he'd meet someone else tonight. He could almost picture himself up there with his arm round a gorgeous girl.

'What are we going on first?' asked Oliver. 'Ghost train might be good.'

Jake looked at him pityingly. Even Megan wasn't impressed.

'You had a knock on the head or something?' she demanded. 'I wouldn't be seen dead on a ghost train!' She giggled. 'If you know what I mean!'

'We're too old for ghost trains,' agreed Jake.

'OK.' Oliver grinned. 'It was just a thought.'

'What about the dodgems?' said Jake. 'They look fast.'

But Megan grabbed their arms and dragged them to the Twister.

'I love this ride,' she said as they piled into one of the capsules. 'Well, I love the look of those guys.' She smiled at the two young men who were taking the money. 'If I ask really nicely, they'll push us round faster.'

The fairground workers were tall, tanned and at least eighteen – and all the girls on the ride seemed to fancy them. Jake couldn't help feeling jealous.

The Twister lurched into life, throwing them all to one end of the seat. Megan made sure she caught the eye of one of the attendants. He sauntered over the undulating floor and gave Megan a wink as he heaved the capsule into a wild spin. Megan shrieked with delight.

When it had finished they staggered off, clutching hold of each other so they didn't fall, and went straight on to the Magic Carpet. Every time the ride plunged down, Jake thought his stomach was going to come out of the top of his head. It was great!

'I'm hungry,' declared Megan, as they swayed down the steps afterwards.

They bought hot dogs, smothered in fried onions and ketchup, and wandered into the mirror maze. It didn't look the most exciting of places but it was something to do while they ate.

They wandered up and down the corridors, watching their endless reflections. Oliver lagged behind, engrossed in his food. Jake and Megan carried on. But when they turned a corner Oliver leaped out in front of them, making Jake drop his hot dog.

'How did you get there so fast?' Jake demanded, looking down at his ruined food.

Oliver waved at them.

'Can't catch me,' came his voice.

Megan ran towards him and crashed into a mirror, smearing it with ketchup.

'It's just his reflection!' she said in amazement.

Jake felt a prod in the back. He turned to see Oliver behind him, beaming like an idiot. Oliver seemed to spend his life thinking up ways of playing tricks on his friends and Jake had fallen for it again.

'Got you both,' laughed Oliver. 'I was behind you all the time.'

They chased him out of the maze.

'That's the last time you catch me out,' Jake grinned. 'What are we going to go on now?'

Megan jumped up and down on the spot. 'I want

to choose again!' she squeaked, pink in the face. She stuck out an arm and spun round wildly. 'And I choose . . .' she looked to see where her finger was pointing, '. . . the fortune-teller!'

Jake looked over. The other rides were newly painted and lit with brilliant-coloured lights. But the fortune-teller's tent was small and shabby. There was a cracked, painted sign over the door which read, 'See Your Future with Madame Destina'. And there was a picture of a white-haired old lady in a shawl and scarf and floaty skirt, peering into a crystal ball.

'We can't go in there,' said Oliver. 'It'll be too embarrassing.'

'But I want to!' squealed Megan. 'It'll be creepy!'

Jake agreed with Oliver. He didn't want to go in but he could see that people were starting to look at Megan. He made a despairing face at his friend above her head.

'Come on,' he said grimly, dragging Megan towards the tent. 'Let's get this over with.'

The inside of the tent was bigger than it had looked from the outside. There was a table covered in an old purple cloth, with one chair behind it and two facing it. An old-fashioned lantern hung from the ceiling, casting an odd light. Megan and Oliver squeezed on to one chair and Jake took the other. There were curtains hanging behind the table, hiding the rest of the tent. They were decorated with signs of the zodiac.

'How cheesy,' muttered Jake. But as he looked at them he began to find the images unpleasant. The Aries ram seemed to be sneering and was that blood on the lion's mane and teeth? He shook his head. He was imagining things. It was just the strange light.

'It's gone very quiet.' Jake found he was whispering. 'I can't hear the fair at all. How weird is that!'

'It's eerie!' Megan whispered back in obvious delight. 'I wonder where Madame Destina is?'

Suddenly the lantern flickered and the back

curtains swished apart as if a performance was starting. There stood the fortune-teller. Jake nearly burst out laughing. Where was the white-haired granny with the rings on her fingers and wart on her nose? This woman was only about twenty. She was wearing skin-tight, pink leather trousers, a T-shirt with the message, 'Don't Bother' and her purple hair gelled up into spikes. She had piercings all over her face. There was no scarf, no shawl and no floaty skirt.

She's a fake, thought Jake.

'Greetings,' the fortune-teller said in a deep, foreign voice. 'And welcome to my tent. I am Madame Destina.' She stared at them fiercely. 'Crystal ball or tarot cards?'

'Tarot cards,' whispered Megan, nervously handing over some money.

Jake sighed heavily. Not the tarot cards.

Madame Destina turned her sharp gaze on him.

'What is the matter, young man?' she asked.

Jake wanted to mutter 'nothing' but to his

surprise he found himself telling Madame Destina the truth! 'It's just that Stacey at school did tarot cards,' he blurted out, 'and it was all mumbo-jumbo and she made everyone shriek by turning over the cards showing the Devil and Death.'

Madame Destina watched him calmly. 'This Stacey did not know how to read the Tarot,' she smiled. But it was not a friendly smile. She took a pack of cards from her pocket, the backs were highly patterned. She shuffled the cards expertly and handed them to Megan.

'Cut the cards,' she ordered. Megan quickly did as she was told and handed the cards back.

Madame Destina had long fingernails, each one intricately painted with moons and stars. Jake watched her pull the cards from the pack in turn and place them on the table, tapping and stroking each one significantly. She solemnly told Megan that she would have a long and happy life, with a wonderful husband and two beautiful children. Megan's eyes were shining by the time she had finished. *The usual stuff*, thought Jake to himself. While Madame Destina gathered up the cards, he saw her eyes flicker on to him for a second, as if she knew what he had been thinking.

Now Oliver had his cards read. Jake shifted in his chair and looked up at the canopy. This was such a load of rubbish. Why couldn't his friends see that Madame Destina was a fraud – he could do just as well himself. Come to think of it, he wouldn't mind getting paid for telling Oliver that he'd have a long life, lots of money and plenty of girlfriends.

Now Madame Destina had finished with Oliver. She turned to Jake and stretched out her hand. He put his pound coin into her palm and watched the painted nails close over the money like claws.

'Go on then, tell me,' he joked. 'Am I going to be an international footballer? Or perhaps a millionaire pop star? Or will I win the lottery on a five-week rollover? What great future is in store for me?'

Madame Destina gave a loud ringing laugh

which stopped as suddenly as it had started.

'I cannot tell your fortune with the Tarot,' she said, without taking her eyes from Jake's face. 'For you do not believe in its power, is that not so?' She did not wait for a reply but slipped a hand into her pocket and slowly drew out a long chain with something furry on the end of it. In the gloomy tent Jake couldn't make out what it was. 'Why do you not decide your own destiny, young man? With this!'

She thrust the dangling chain at him. A dirty, moth-eaten rabbit's foot swung slowly in his face. Jake had seen this sort of thing before. You had to hold it in your hand and make a wish, which was sure to come true, or so it was said. Jake had always thought this was unlikely. After all, the rabbit hadn't had much luck, had it?

As he put his hand out, Jake hesitated. No way did he want to touch that flea-bitten scrap of fur!

Plus, there was something about this fortune-teller that made Jake uncomfortable. Her eyes seemed to see right inside his head. But Jake knew there was something he was desperate to wish for. He reached forward and grabbed the rabbit's foot.

It felt cold and worn and stiff in his hand. He shut his eyes, took a deep breath and was just about to make his wish when Madame Destina suddenly snatched the foot back from him and held up a warning hand.

'Wait,' she said sharply. 'Do not be in such a hurry. You must be careful what you wish for.'

Jake tutted and rolled his eyes. 'I promise,' he said impatiently.

He put his hand over the rabbit's foot and silently made his wish. Suddenly the foot felt warm in his hand. He was sure it twitched. It felt alive!

Jake leaped to his feet, knocking his chair flying. Madame Destina was staring fixedly at him. *She knows what I wished*, he thought. *She knows!*

The fortune-teller raised an eyebrow.

'Have a nice life,' she said simply.

Jake stumbled backwards, felt the door flap behind him and scrambled through it. The noise of the fair hit him and he stood gulping in the night air.

Now he was out of the tent, he felt embarrassed at the fuss he'd made. Of course the rabbit's foot wasn't alive. It didn't have a rabbit attached to it! But he felt like that woman had been inside his head and he had to shake her out.

Megan and Oliver joined him.

'Are you all right?' asked Oliver, puzzled. 'You've gone a bit pale.'

'I'm fine,' Jake told him. 'Why wouldn't I be?' He gave his friends a wobbly smile. 'Can we have some proper fun now?'

'The ghost train,' said Oliver firmly. 'It's my turn to choose. Megan wanted the fortune-teller and Twister and you got to pick the Magic Carpet. And I want to go on the ghost train.'

Jake stared open-mouthed at his friend. He couldn't believe Oliver was suggesting the ghost train again. But he could see that Oliver wasn't joking. Jake gave up.

'Let's get it over and done with then,' he said.

The entrance to the ghost train was festooned with green lights and waving skeletons. Distant mechanical groans wafted out of the dark tunnel. Jake looked around as they paid for their tickets. They were the only ones there and he didn't want anyone from school seeing him go on such a silly ride. He knew he shouldn't care what people thought but he couldn't help it.

They climbed on to the ghost train. Megan and Oliver dashed straight to the double seat at the back. Jake was sure that Megan was going to shriek like a baby so he went and sat at the front, as far away from them as he could.

The train slowly moved towards the swinging double doors. With a jolt it pushed them open and rattled off into the tunnel and total darkness. The mechanical groaning was louder now.

'Here we go!' Jake said to himself with a grin. 'Into the mouth of Hell!'

The first thing he noticed was a cold breeze and a foul smell, like bad drains.

The train moved suddenly round a corner and now there was a faint red light. Not very scary either – he could see the string of red bulbs hanging from the ceiling. They were meant to be hidden in cobwebs but most of the webs had fallen away. There was a silly howling sound and a plastic mummy with trailing bandages lurched towards him and then sprang back to lurch again at the car behind. There seemed to be something red running down the walls.

Jake turned round. 'Great ride!' he shouted back to Megan and Oliver. 'Look at the blood – it's more like strawberry ice cream!'

A bat fluttered over his head. Jake could clearly see the string. He wished he had some scissors. The train suddenly turned a sharp corner and a cardboard ghost lurched out at him.

'Whoooo!' he heard Megan wail and then shriek with laughter.

'Having a good time, Jake?' called Oliver cheerfully. 'Sure you're not scared up there all on your own?'

'Don't worry,' Jake grinned back. 'I'm tough!'

The train clattered on and suddenly went down a slope. There were still the usual rubbish ghosts and vampires but now in between them there were other objects. Things that shouldn't be in a ghost train. Jake began to feel a bit puzzled. First there was a grandfather clock with its hands circling furiously and then around the curve of the tunnel there was a strange video projection showing the sun chasing the moon at great speed.

Someone's put them in the wrong ride, thought Jake.

There was another jolt and the ride picked up speed. Giant watches whizzed by, ticking wildly. Jake began to feel uneasy. This wasn't like any ghost train he'd been on before. Music started to blare all around him. It was harsh music with crashing chords and sounded as if it was being played way too fast. And the smell! It was getting stronger and stronger. 'Phew!' Jake called back. 'They really do have a problem with their drains.' But Oliver and Megan didn't reply. They probably couldn't hear him over the loud music.

A huge digital clock now seemed to block the way of the car. Its numbers were running so quickly they were a blur of light. Just when Jake thought he would crash into it the car lurched to the side and hurtled down another slope.

A lolling plastic Dracula came into view. But strangely, a giant egg-timer burst out from behind it. It was turning over and over in the air, and Jake couldn't see any strings. The sand inside was being thrown about. But it wasn't sand. It looked more like blood sloshing in there, and real blood this time. Jake knew it couldn't be.

All of a sudden a huge black pendulum swung straight at his head. Jake was sure it was going to smash into him. He ducked.

What was going on? This ride was like some sort of dream. The music was deafening and he thought he'd be sick with the smell. He'd never been on a ghost train like this in his life. It was showing no signs of coming to an end. If anything it was going even faster and plummeting down again, throwing Jake back in his seat. When would it go back up? They must be miles underground by now.

Jake was desperate for the ride to end. He looked down at his watch and pressed the illumination button. To his astonishment his watch was going mad. The hands were whirring through the hours just like all the clocks on the ride! How could the ride make that happen? Jake swivelled round in his seat to shout back at Oliver and Megan and ask if their watches were doing the same.

Jake knelt on the seat and tried to look back. The tunnel was full of clock faces flashing by. The discordant music had stopped but now all around him were pings and beeps, clangs and chimes, impossibly loud. Their different rhythms collided with each other, hurting his ears. The train was speeding along now and he had to cling on to the back of the car to keep his balance. He couldn't see anything. He struggled up to stand on the seat. Now the whole train was stretched out behind. He could see all the way to the end car. He couldn't believe his eyes. Megan and Oliver weren't there! The train was completely empty. He was the only person on the ride!

Jake felt a sudden blow on the back of his head and he was thrown into the next car. For a few minutes he lay there stunned. He must have hit his head on the roof of the tunnel. His whole body ached, especially his chest. Had he broken a rib in the fall? Each breath made him gasp in agony and he could feel his heart pounding.

'Aargh!' he groaned as he pulled himself up on to the seat. His hand hurt like mad and it was oozing with blood. As he tried to wipe it away, his skin wrinkled like dry paper and he saw in the dim light that his hands were shaking. Then he noticed his nails. They looked thick and ugly and yellow.

And now the cold breeze was cutting through him. It seemed to get right into his joints. He shivered and wrapped his arms round his chest.

He was stuck in this terrible ride, hurtling through the dark. Surely someone must be around to rescue him!

'Help!' he shouted. 'Someone get me out of here!' But his voice came out as a pathetic croak.

If only Oliver and Megan were there. He couldn't understand how they had disappeared.

Then it dawned on him. Oliver had tricked him again! Just like in the maze of mirrors. Just like he always did. That's why he'd been so determined to go on the ride. He'd been very clever. But this time he had gone too far. Jake was in real pain, and that wasn't funny.

At last the ride slowed down. Jake could see a slit of light ahead. *At last this nightmare is coming to an end*, he thought desperately. But as the train reached the doors a terrifying, hooded figure loomed up in

front of him. It held a scythe and pointed at him
with a skeletal hand. From the hood two glowing
eyes burned into him and the tunnel echoed with
the sound of a deep, hollow laugh. Jake cowered
back in his seat.

The car slowly clattered out from the tunnel and
ground to a halt. Jake could see Oliver and Megan
looking round for him as if he'd got lost.

Great acting, he thought sourly. *Well, I'll show them.
I'll make as if nothing's happened.*

Megan glanced over at the ghost train and then
turned away as if she didn't recognize him. Jake
began to climb out, slowly and painfully. An
attendant rushed over and offered to help.
Jake found himself gratefully leaning on the
attendant's arm.

He tried to straighten his shoulders and march
over to his friends as if nothing was wrong, but
every joint in his body ached as he moved. He felt
worse than he had ever done in his life! He slowly

shuffled along. Oliver and Megan were looking straight at him now, but they didn't seem to recognize him.

Then suddenly Megan's eyes widened with shock. She nudged Oliver urgently and pointed at Jake.

'Jake!' she whispered. She looked him up and down. 'It can't be you, can it?'

'Course it's me.' Jake immediately burst into a fit of coughing. There was something wrong with his voice. It sounded raspy and high.

'What's happened?' asked Oliver. He was pretending to look scared.

'Your joke didn't work,' said Jake hoarsely. 'That's what happened. I was all alone on the ghost train like you planned but I wasn't scared, so bad luck!'

'What joke?' said Oliver.

'Jake . . . you're . . . you're . . .' Megan was crying now. Jake couldn't believe it. The girl deserved an Oscar!

'A bit bruised?' he croaked. 'A bit knocked about?

Is that what you're trying to say? Well, I'm not surprised. I got badly hurt thanks to your stupid joke!'

Oliver tried to smile. 'A trick,' he gasped. 'That's it. *You're* playing a trick on *us*. But I can't work out how you're doing it. It looks so *real*.'

What were they going on about? Jake began to shake with anger. Oliver was the one who'd had a trick played on him. He was the one who had got hurt because of them. But Oliver and Megan looked truly scared. What on earth was happening?

Jake looked down at his hands. In the bright lights of the fair they were horrible, wrinkled and dry with brown mottled patches. His fingers were bent and his knuckles looked swollen. He tried to think straight but his ears were still ringing from the blow on the head and it was difficult to concentrate. His eyes were so blurry that when he peered at Megan, he had to screw them up to focus properly on her.

All Jake's anger suddenly drained out of him. Now he was just tired – and scared.

'I don't understand,' he whimpered. 'I'm not playing any tricks.'

Megan and Oliver looked at each other. Their faces were white. They each took an arm and led him slowly over to the mirror maze.

They stopped in front of the first mirror.

Jake didn't recognize the person in the reflection. He was wearing the same T-shirt as Jake had put on to go to the nightclub earlier that evening. He had the same trainers and jeans as Jake. But there was no sign of Jake's carefully gelled haircut, just snowy white strands of hair spread thinly over a bald head. The wrinkled old face had broken veins across its cheeks. The man in the mirror was bent as if he couldn't straighten his shoulders. His clothes hung off him.

Jake peered closer. The old man in the mirror did the same. Jake shuffled his feet. The reflection copied. Jake put his fingers up to his face, so did the reflection. Under his fingers he could feel rough skin and sharp, bristly hairs that needed a shave.

Jake was looking at himself.

I want to be older and I want it now, he'd wished. The fortune-teller had made his wish come true – with the help of the rabbit's foot. But she'd got it wrong! Hadn't she understood? He had only wanted to be a bit older so that he could get along with girls and make them fancy him. The rabbit's foot had granted his wish – too literally.

Jake could feel his heart pounding in his ears. He stared at his reflection in the mirror. His lips were blue.

Madame Destina had warned him to be careful what he wished for. He needed one more wish – to have his time back.

But then a crushing pain shot across his chest. As he collapsed on the ground he knew that time was the one thing he didn't have.

Terrify yourself with more books from Nick Shadow's
Midnight Library

Vol. I: *Voices*
Kate knows that something is wrong when she starts hearing voices in her head. But she doesn't know what the voices mean, or what terror they will lead her to . . .

Vol. II: *Blood and Sand*
John and Sarah are on the most boring seaside holiday of their lives. And when they come up against the sinister Sandman, they really begin to wish they'd stayed at home . . .

Vol. III: *The Cat Lady*
Chloe never quite believed her friend's stories about the Cat Lady. But when a dare goes horribly wrong, she finds out that the truth is more terrifying than anyone had ever imagined . . .

Terrify yourself with more books from Nick Shadow's
Midnight Library

Vol. IV: *The Cat Lady*

Chloe never quite believed her friend's stories about the Cat Lady. But when a dare goes horribly wrong, she finds out that the truth is more terrifying than anyone had ever imagined . . .

Vol. V: *Liar*

Lauren is shy. She just wants a friend, and she's so lonely she even imagined herself one. But she soon realizes she's created a monster. A monster called Jennifer . . .

Vol. VI: *Shut your Mouth*

Louise and her mates love to get their sweets from Mr Webster's old-fashioned shop, but when their plan to get some of the new 'Special Delights' goes wrong, could they have bitten off more than they can chew?